Marisa's Recurring Nightmares

Presented by
The Great Lakes Association of
Horror Writers

Based on an idea by
Ken MacGregor

Edited by
J. M. Van Horn

www.glahw.com

ISBN: 9798686380226

This anthology is a work of fiction. With the exclusion of the name "Marisa," names, characters, places, and scenarios are the products of the authors' imagination. Any resemblance to actual persons living or dead, places, or events is purely coincidental. "Marisa" has been used by permission with our deepest gratitude and disturbing glee.

Collection and editorial content
Copyright © Great Lakes Association of Horror Writers 2020

Cover art copyright © Steven J. Bejma 2020

Great Lakes Association of Horror Writers logo by Dave Harvey
Copyright © Great Lakes Association of Horror Writers 2007

All rights reserved. No portion of this publication can be reproduced by any means without the prior written permission from the authors of the work and from the Great Lakes Association of Horror Writers.

THE DIVINE RELEASE copyright © 2020 Peggy Christie
GARDEN OF SECRETS copyright © 2020 R D Doan
UNNERVED copyright © 2020 Max Carrey
MARISA'S CURSE copyright © 2020 Clark Roberts
MARISA'S STATUE copyright © 2020 Radar DeBoard
LITTLE GARDEN GNOMES copyright © 2020 Aaron Grierson
THE BIZZ OF A FLY copyright © 2020 David Allen Voyles
REFUGE copyright © 2020 Elias Baum
THE WHITE LADY copyright © 2020 Zachary Finn
LULLABY OF HIGHBANK RIDGE copyright © 2020 Jen Sexton-Riley
ROAD FLARES copyright © 2020 Neil Willoughby

CONTENTS

AN INTRODUCTION
The Divine Release 1
   by Peggy Christie
Garden of Secrets 17
   by R D Doan
Unnerved 25
   by Max Carrey
Marisa's Curse 33
   by Clark Roberts
Marisa's Statue 45
   by Radar DeBoard
Little Garden Gnomes 51
   by Aaron Grierson
The Buzz of a Fly 65
   by David Allen Voyles
Refuge 75
   by Elias Baum
The White Lady 83
   by Zachary Finn
Lullaby of Highbank Bridge 93
   by Jen Sexton-Riley
Road Flares 103
   By Neil Willoughby
Baku 117
About GLAHW 121

AN INTRODUCTION

My name is J.M. Van Horn and I was given an amazing opportunity to take up the role as editor for a unique project. One of GLAHW's annual anthologies, the Recurring Nightmares.

The project began as a simple one. It started in 2013 when Ken MacGregor came up with the brilliant idea for a special auction prize at our annual Monster Mash for Literacy Bash to raise money for the Dominican Literacy Center. The raffle offered folks a way to help others transform their lives.

In return, the owner of the winning ticket earned something special. Their name would become the focus of the contributing author's stories. Hero, villain, victim, or monster. It was up to the author in how they used them.

As an added bonus to task the author's creative skills, they were asked to include something special to the winner. Previous items had been dogs or a travelling circus.

Our most recent raffle winner was selected and our authors had a name for their upcoming inspiration, Marisa. The only other requirement the winner set was a garden statue had to be involved.

When it was all said and done, there were eleven talented authors who crafted tales you are sure to remember when you hear the name *Marisa*.

Welcome to her nightmares.

J.M. Van Horn
Editor, Fall 2020

nighty-night
 don't let the bed bugs bite

THE DIVINE RELEASE
by Peggy Christie

Marisa bolted up in bed. At first, she couldn't remember where she was. After working in the garden all afternoon, she'd fallen into a heavy slumber minutes after her head hit the pillow. But as the web of sleep fell away, she recognized the familiar shapes and corners of her bedroom.

She laid back on her pillows, sleep already taking over again, when the echo of breaking glass shook her. Any remaining film of sleep disappeared as Marisa imagined who or what had broken into her house.

Marisa slipped from beneath the safety of the warm comforter, and inched toward the open bedroom door. Standing in the dark, she listened for additional noises, soon chiding herself for being such a coward. Her sister, Marie, used to tease her all the time about her nervous nature. Marisa inhaled then strode through the hall, down the stairs, and into the kitchen. She noted the open window above the sink, the evening breeze rustling the curtain.

"I thought I closed that."

She clicked on the light and moved to the window. Shards from two broken glasses laid in the sink. She'd put them on the counter after she and Marie shared some lemonade this afternoon, *before* their weekly argument. Perhaps the wind blew them over. Marisa stepped away from the sink and turned toward the storage closet for an old rag to pick up the broken glass.

She saw a shadow figure in the corner by the back door, and screamed.

"Who are you?"

The figure didn't respond, and she took a shaky step forward. "Who-?"

She could now see the upturned tail, thick layers of scales, and two round bulbous eyes - her koi statue from the garden. Confusion replaced fear.

"How'd you get in here?"

She reached around it and twisted the doorknob. It swung open. She imagined every possible scenario, but no logic could support the idea of an intruder. Who would break in just to leave the statue here?

Marisa slipped on a pair of flip flops near the back door, then picked up the statue. It only came up to her knees, but its diminutive size belied its heft. She struggled to move it across the concrete patio. Tilting it on the edge of its base, she rolled it across the cement to the grass.

Lugging it to the back corner of the yard, toward her modest garden, the full moon lit up the way. A matted path ran through the grass between the garden and the house. Marisa stopped to examine it, her breath labored. If she didn't know better, she would have believed the fish statue dragged itself to the house.

Marisa shook her head and continued to haul it back to its proper place, huffing with irritation.

"Someone's playing a prank. Probably those Jencks children."

Her neighbors next door had two boys, notorious troublemakers. She made a mental note to speak to their mother in the morning.

Once she got the statue back in place, she patted its tail.

"Don't worry, Em. I'll make sure those hooligans don't bother you again."

The next morning, Marisa shuffled downstairs to make coffee. She'd almost forgotten about the statue, but once she saw the remnants of glass still in the sink, her head began to ache. Just something else to deal with on a day already filled with errands.

"Well, I can't do anything before breakfast."

Once she fortified herself with a pot of coffee, a full meal, and a hot shower, Marisa decided to talk to Mrs. Jencks now. After slipping into her tennis shoes, Marisa headed out the front door and turned right, cutting through the yard until she arrived on the doorstep of the Jencks' house. She rang the doorbell, then quickly ran her hands through her hair and pulled at her unzipped jacket, smoothing her appearance as best as possible.

She could hear Marie's scolding voice. *"Pull yourself together, Marisa."*

When no one answered, she rang the bell again. She heard a muffled, "I'm coming!" from inside seconds before a haggard and disheveled Cordy Jencks opened the door. The dark circles under her eyes stood out against her pale skin; a messy bun of hair sagged near her left ear; her misbuttoned blouse hung untucked over a stained pair of pale pink sweatpants. Mrs. Jencks grimaced.

"What is it now, Marisa?"

"I'm sorry to bother you, Cordy, but I wanted to talk to you about your boys."

"My boys? You mean the two who have been stuck home with the flu for the past three days, who have been throwing up nonstop, but somehow still fighting like cats and dogs, draining me of any remaining will to live? You mean those boys?"

Cordy's voice became shrill as it coiled into a high screech. As she glared at Marisa, daring her to continue, Marisa heard heavy retching sounds as one of the boys raced past Cordy and up the stairs. The woman turned her head to watch him, and her shoulders sagged in exhaustion.

"Never mind, Cordy. I'm obviously mistaken about something. I won't bother you-"

Cordy slammed the door and shouted, "Good!"

Marisa leaned back as a rush of air hit her face. She stepped off the porch, and headed back home. The Jencks' boys hadn't toyed with the statue, leaving Marisa perplexed. She walked back toward her driveway, chewing on her lower lip. She caught a flash in her peripheral vision and looked left. Leaning against the chain link fence sat the statue, the flexible wire bulging outward under its weight.

"What?"

She jogged over to the fence. Someone had placed it here in a rush, as if they tried to steal it before Marisa returned. Maybe they were still here.

Scrabbling over the fence, she caught her jeans on one of the wire ends along the top rail. It tore through the fabric, gouging the top of her thigh. She cried out as she flopped onto the ground next to the statue. She stood on shaky legs then hobbled toward the corner of her house. Unfortunately, she didn't see the perpetrator on her property.

She didn't have time to replace the sculpture now. It would take too long to move it, and she had an appointment in twenty minutes. That didn't give her much time to change clothes and dress her wound. Sighing, Marisa patted its tail.

"Sorry, Em. Can you wait for me? I'll get you back to the garden as soon as I can."

She chuckled at her own joke. Of course it could wait. Her amusement died, though, as she considered that the statue relocated on its own. She shook her head, dismissing the idea. But as she limped inside to change, a nagging kernel of doubt took root in her mind.

After returning home hours later, Marisa put the kettle on for tea. While it warmed, she would move the statue. Her leg ached, but didn't think it would hinder her efforts. Moving outside, she almost plowed into Em on the patio.

"What are you doing here? Didn't I leave you–"

"No."

Marisa froze as she heard a soft, lyrical voice come from the fish.

"Excuse me?"

"No, you didn't leave me there, Marisa. Walter did."

"Walter, the man next door? That Walter?"

"Yes."

"That's silly. Why?"

"He likes to watch you."

"Watch me do what?"

"Anything. Everything. Moving me around was just an excuse to get you out in the open. Made it easier for him."

"I don't…do you mean he watches me inside, too?"

"Yes, when he can catch you at a window. He has little patience, though."

Marisa clutched her sweater at her throat, her eyes darting back and forth. The shed on her right blocked the view from Walter's house, so she scurried to it and pressed her back against it.

"Is he looking now?"

"No, but he will soon. He planned to move me again, not just to make you come outside, but to make you think you're going crazy."

She frowned as she approached the fish. "So if he didn't put you here…"

"That's right. I moved on my own. I couldn't let Walter mess with you again."

"Did he put you in the house? Did he break the glasses?"

"Yes."

Marisa's hands flew to her mouth in horror. She'd never thought much about Walter. He kept to himself, said hello from time to time. She always viewed him as a loner, not a pervert.

But those are usually the troubled ones. Watch any news program about a serial killer or psycho, and it's the same story.

"*He was always so quiet.*"

"*Never bothered anyone.*"

"*Hardly ever saw him.*"

Marisa stared at the koi, chewing on her fingernail. "But what can I do? I can't tell the police you told me."

"True, but you could make an anonymous report about him."

Marisa smiled. "Good idea. They get anonymous tips all the time. But they'll trace it back to me."

"Not if you use the pay phone at the mall."

Marisa snapped her fingers. "Of course. Em, you're a genius."

"Just tell the police that you've witnessed Walter going into people's yards at night, looking in their windows."

"Oh, I can't believe someone like him lives next door." She stared down at the statue. "Do you want to go back in the garden?"

"Do you want me to go back in the garden?"

"I think I'd feel better if you came in the house."

"Of course, Marisa. Help me."

"Say no more."

Marisa dragged the statue into the kitchen, setting it to rest near the door. Wheezing, Marisa smiled.

"Is this good?"

"For now. I can see out the back door, guard for trouble. You just go make that call."

"Back in a jiffy."

Marisa slipped out the front door, keeping her gaze on Walter's house. As she drove away, she saw his car pull into his driveway. Though she considered turning around, she needed to report Walter as soon as possible, and trusted Em to keep a lookout for any further suspicious activity.

Marisa parked near the east entrance of the mall. The only payphone she knew to exist in the area stood alone and unused outside those doors. She picked up the receiver and pressed 9-1-1. The dial tone changed to ringing, and within a few seconds, an operator answered.

"9-1-1, what's your emergency?"

"I'd like to report a peeping Tom."

"A peeping Tom?"

"Yes. I've been taking evening walks in my neighborhood, and I've seen a man peeping through people's windows or sneaking into their backyards."

"Do you know this individual?"

"Yes, ma'am, I do. I've seen him go into the house at 3529 Lakewood many times. That's in Troy, by the way. I assume it's his home."

"Is he there now?"

"I can't say for sure. He was there fifteen minutes ago."

"I understand. I'll dispatch an officer immediately. What is your na-?"

Marisa hung up the phone. She needed to get back before the police showed up. They couldn't connect her to the call if they traced it here while she sat in her living room.

Pushing her car far above the speed limit, she made it home in less than ten minutes. The authorities hadn't arrived yet. As she rushed inside her house, Em stood in the room to her right, a few feet away from the bay window. Marisa squeaked in surprise.

"What are you doing there? I though you wanted to watch from the back door."

"Will the police arrive out front?"

"They should. Can you let me know when they come? I need to make some tea."

"Yes."

Marisa hurried into the kitchen, readying a cup and tea bag as she waited for the water to heat. She giggled with anticipation. When she returned to the sitting room, she eased herself into a high-backed chair, and gawked out the window.

"Anything yet?"

"No."

Just then a dark blue sedan, with "Troy Police" printed in white block letters across the doors, parked in front of Walter's house. Two officers exited the vehicle, a short petite woman in her thirties, and a tall, muscular man around the same age. The woman spoke into a walkie on her shoulder as they both approached Walter's house.

Marisa saw two neighbors across the street come out of their homes, each standing on their respective porches, watching the event unfold.

"I'm going outside, Em. I want to hear what happens."

"I'll observe from here."

Marisa stood on her porch, gripping the hot cup of tea in her hands, feigning as much worry as she could muster. She heard footsteps. Cordy Jencks approached, wearing clean clothes, makeup, her hair secured in a sleek ponytail.

"Do you know what's going on?"

"Not yet. I just saw them pull up."

Cordy nodded, and rubbed the back of her neck. "Look, I'm really sorry for snapping at you this morning. I haven't slept well in days."

"You don't have to apologize. I completely understand. And I'm sorry I almost accused your boys of…well, it doesn't matter."

Cordy smiled, and they watched the police ring Walter's doorbell.

"I wonder what they want with Walter. The man never says boo to anyone."

"Yeah, he's always so quiet, right?" Cordy said.

Marisa bit her lip to avoid laughing. More neighbors stood on their porches to study the growing spectacle. As their questioning continued, the woman's hand shot up, quieting both men. Marisa watched as she progressed into Walter's house, unsnapping her gun holster. Her partner gripped Walter's arm then pulled him to the side.

Within a few minutes, the female officer burst through the door, yelling.

"Mark, get cuffs on that guy right now! There are at least three women restrained in one of the bedrooms. I'll call for backup."

The male officer's expression morphed from surprise to confusion to determination in a matter of seconds. He handcuffed Walter before his partner got to their car, and secured him in the backseat by the time she'd finished.

"Stay with him. I'll free those women, then do a quick search for anyone else."

"You're not going in alone. Besides," he said as he swept his arm through the air. "The neighbors won't let him escape."

Two men from across the street stepped forward, and one called out. "We can keep an eye on him. Do what you have to do."

The male officer nodded, removed his gun from its holster,

then followed his partner back into the house. Marisa looked at Cordy.

"Did she say women were tied up in Walter's house?"

"I can't believe it, but yeah, she did."

"Wow, you just never know, do you?"

"You can say that again."

Marisa hid a smile behind the cup of tea she brought to her lips. Ten minutes later, three more squad cars arrived, and within an hour, police rescued eight different women from the home. The emaciated victims, filthy, bruised, and terrified, cried and held each other as several ambulances took them to the local hospital.

The evening news related the story of Walter Rogers, former Army Captain, retired from GM, widower, father of two grown boys, and grandfather to five. The investigation outed a once quiet and respected member of the community as a kidnapper, rapist, and torturer of eight women, murderer of three, and now a suspect in the cases of four missing women. Marisa studied the television broadcast, shaking her head as she nibbled Oreo cookies.

"It's always the quiet ones. That's what Marie always said."

She glanced at the koi in the corner of the room. "You knew he wasn't just a peeper, didn't you?"

"I did. I thought you wouldn't believe me. I'm sure a talking statue frightened you enough, let alone discovering a murderer lived next door."

"That probably was for the best. And I appreciate it."

Once the broadcast ended, Marisa turned off the tv. She stretched her arms over her head and looked at the clock.

"I'm tired. It's been a busy day. See you in the morning, Em."

"Sleep well, Marisa."

The next morning, the koi greeted Marisa as she walked into the kitchen. "Good morning. Did you sleep well?"

Marisa squeaked in surprise, then laughed as she pressed her hand against her chest. "I forgot you were in here, Em. You sounded just like my sister."

"Understandable."

"I think I slept better than I have in a long time. Great peace of mind comes with knowing that man can't hurt anyone anymore."

"True, but you didn't think he was the only one, did you?"

Marisa stood at the open refrigerator door, the gallon of milk in her hand as she stared at the statue.

"You did a good thing, but there's a lot more evil in this neighborhood."

Marisa felt her hands tremble and she returned the milk to the fridge. "Like what?"

By the time Marisa finished breakfast, Em had revealed the crimes of the McPheresons across the street. Marisa never paid them much attention, except that they seemed a little *too* happy, a little *too* perfect. According to the koi, the couple ran an illegal gambling racket out of their basement.

"How? They have young children, teenagers, whose friends visit all the time."

"Who do you think they're trapping into the gambling life? They need to get them young, just like drug dealers."

"That's terrible. Maybe I should make another anonymous call to law enforcement."

"I would."

The arrest of Jewel and James created a frenzy of activity, as did Social Services when they rounded up the kids. Neighbors stood on their porches, shaking their heads at the spectacle. Marisa had no proof other than Em's word, but that would change after an official investigation.

Within the week, Marisa ratted out three more families on her street. By the end of the month, authorities arrested four others from the blocks bordering hers. The statue gave her details of each family's crimes, from drugs to human trafficking to tax evasion. She knew the police would find the evidence needed to convict them all. But getting them into custody first meant their evils could be stamped out sooner rather than later.

One evening, with the echoes of sirens filling the night air, Marisa sat on Cordy's porch, sipping tea with her neighbor. Cordy's voice shook with worry.

"I don't know what's going on in this neighborhood, but either we do have a lot of bad elements around here or someone's paranoia has hit DEFCON 1."

"Seems to me to be the first. How could all these people get apprehended if they weren't guilty?"

"Where's the proof? I mean, they found Walter's dirty little secret right away. But the rest? All but one have come home, proven innocent, but now everyone looks at them sideways. Like, just the accusation was enough to ruin them, you know?"

"Unless they're already ruined."

"Huh?"

"Maybe whomever is reporting them has proof, but is afraid the suspects might take revenge on her."

"Her? Marisa, do you know something about all this?"

Marisa looked at Cordy, and took a deep breath. "Can I trust you?"

Cordy's eyes widened. Not with dread, but greedy anticipation. "Of course, Marisa. Tell me what you know."

"I think it's better if I show you."

Marisa put the teacup down and stood. "Follow me."

She led Cordy over to her house and through the front door. She'd left Em near the bay window to observe the neighborhood. Only an empty room greeted them. Marisa scratched her head.

"Huh, I left her here. Maybe she's in the kitchen."

"Uh, Marisa?"

"Don't worry, I'll find her."

Still no Em, until she looked out the kitchen window. "Ah, she's out back. C'mon."

"What's going on?"

Marisa led Cordy to the garden in the far-left corner. Cordy frowned.

"Who did you want to show me?"

"Her," Marisa pointed at the koi.

Cordy stared from the statue to Marisa and back again. "I don't get it."

Marisa checked over both her shoulders before whispering. "The statue told me everything."

Cordy straightened and crossed her arms. "The *statue* told you?"

"She knew about Walter. She has the goods on everyone around here."

"I see. So, she talks to you?"

"Of course."

"Uh huh. Will she talk to me?"

"Ask her something."

Cordy bent toward the statue. "Um, excuse me, Miss Fish. What can you tell me about the Anderson bunch on Balmoral?"

The statue didn't respond. Marisa frowned.

"Em, tell her what you know."

The fish remained silent. Cordy gave Marisa a sidelong glance as she straightened. "I think I should get back. Spence and the kids must be waiting on dinner."

"But don't you want to talk to her?"

"Maybe she doesn't trust me, haha."

Marisa frowned at Cordy and stepped backward. She leaned toward the statue.

"Is that why you won't talk, Em?"

Cordy raised her hands, a nervous laugh echoing around them. "I'm not a bad guy. I swear. Come on, Marisa. You know me."

"Do I?"

Cordy spun on her heel and jogged to the backyard gate. She let herself out of Marisa's yard, continually looking over her shoulder. Marisa scrutinized the dark, even after Cordy disappeared from sight. She glowered at the gate, but spoke to the statue.

"Is Cordy's bad, too?"

"Yes, Marisa. I wasn't sure until just now. I could smell the evil on her."

"Okay, what can you tell me?"

Cordy burst through her front door, scaring her husband and kids. They were sitting at the kitchen table, waiting on her to make dinner. The boys stared at her with wide eyes as she raced toward the phone. Her husband moved beside her, placing a hand on her shoulder.

"Hon, are you okay? You look like you've seen a ghost."

"I've seen worse than that, Spence. I've just seen what bat shit crazy looks like up close. I gotta call the cops."

"What happened?"

"Marisa Fenton, that's what happened. Hello? Yes, my name is Cordelia Jencks. I live at 3525 Lakewood. My neighbor has been reporting all the 'bad people' around here because she said her garden statue told her to."

Cordy gazed at her husband while the operator transferred her call. Spence arched an eyebrow. She grimaced at him as a gruff voice sounded through the phone.

"This is Lieutenant Hobbes. Are you calling in regard to a Marisa Fenton?"

"Yes, sir. And she just told me how she found out about everyone's crimes."

"After the first few reports, we began to suspect her. We couldn't be sure, as no phone records exist, linking her residence to the calls. Do you think you could come down to the station and meet with me?"

"I'd be more than happy to. I might be her next target."

"When can you come in?"

"Fifteen minutes?"

"I'll be waiting. Thank you, Mrs. Jencks."

Cordy hung up the phone and turned to her family. "You guys can either wait for me or just order a pizza. I'll fill you in when I get back."

She kissed her bewildered husband on the cheek, grabbed her purse, and ran out the door. As she got into her car, she could see Marisa standing in her bay window, binoculars in hand. Cordy could hardly steady her keys to get them in the ignition. The tires squealed as she raced to the local police station.

The following morning, Lieutenant Hobbes assumed he stood in Marisa's kitchen, as he couldn't see one clean surface to confirm it. Shards of broken glass laid in the sink, several pieces covered in a dried, brown film; shaky towers of dirty dishes covered the counters and stove; crusty towels and napkins littered the floor and kitchen table; fast food bags created a greasy, mold-covered mountain in the corner.

In the room with the large bay window, sheets of paper lined the walls from floor to ceiling, each covered in nonsensible scrawls. A dry erase board leaned on an easel near the window, its entire surface colored in with red marker. A small table held binoculars, dirty teacups, a scattering of dull pencils and inkless pens, and notebooks filled with more random scribbles.

One of the rookie uniformed officers rushed into the house, red faced and sweating. "Lieutenant, you gotta come see this."

He led Hobbes into the back yard. An overgrown, weed infested garden sat in the back-left corner of the yard, and the lawn consisted of muddy pits and yellowed grass. That explained the fresh and dried trails of muck that wound through the whole house. The rookie stood next to the small shed on the right.

As Hobbes approached, another officer opened the two shed doors, and a large collection of garbage bags spilled out onto the grass. Hobbes threw his arm up over his mouth and nose, and wretched, twisting away from the rotting refuse and the stink. Two of the other cops gagged, and one threw up.

Hobbes took another whiff, and he frowned. His queasy stomach forgotten, he straightened and stepped closer to the door.

"Haskill, Robinson. Get over here. We need to clear this mess out now."

"What is it?"

Hobbes turned to Robinson. "Haven't you ever smelled anything like this before, kid?"

"No, sir."

"Then maybe you should sit this one out. Nichols, over here."

The three men heaved garbage bags left and right, some splitting open and splashing various unidentifiable liquids over their clothing. Hobbes didn't care. He'd never forgotten the sweet, sickening stench of rotting flesh of the first homicide victim he'd ever encountered.

After clearing out half of the bags, the odor hit them full force and all three vomited.

"What is it, sir?" Robinson asked.

When Hobbes finished puking, he stumbled onto the patio. He pointed at Robinson then motioned toward the front of the house.

"Get on the radio, and call for backup. We found two bodies."

Pale and shaking, Robinson ran to his squad car with no further questions.

When the sun rose the next morning, Marisa's back yard looked like an archaeological site. Forensics roped off half a dozen sections, and dug them up. Aside from the two corpses in the shed, they found two more buried in the yard, and one in the garden. Hobbes conferred with an FBI agent inside the house, while two others guarded a handcuffed Marisa, who slumped in defeat on the couch.

"My guess is she was ratting out her neighbors to keep any attention off herself, though she did get lucky with that Walter guy. So what makes you think the body from the garden is the oldest?"

The agent scribbled notes in a small book. "According to forensics, it was the most decomposed. Some visible bones, a lot of the flesh had already begun to dry. Adult female, buried under that statue. Could be why she thought it spoke to her in woman's voice."

"Guilt does crazy stuff to the head."

"That'll be for the psychologists to figure out, I suppose. She have any family?"

"A sister, Marie. But we haven't been able to get a hold of her yet."

The agent nodded, and Hobbes sipped cold coffee. He watched with an exhausted interest as medical personnel bagged samples of everything from Marisa's clothing to the broken glass in the sink. He noted fresh dirt tracks on the carpet then excused himself from the agent. Pushing his way through the crowd, Hobbes shouted.

"Anyone not *actively* working, get the hell out. There's enough here for forensics to test. You adding to it won't do anyone any favors, got it?"

A handful of uniformed officers and techs in civilian clothing left through the front door, followed by the agents and Marisa Fenton. Hobbes pushed through the back door. More people stood around, gossiping or walking the scene.

"Hey! You people get back to the station. There's plenty of paperwork to fill out, right?"

A jumble of affirmatives answered him as the group left the yard. Hobbes walked toward the garden and the two forensic technicians packing up their equipment. One nodded as he moved away, the other smiled at Hobbes.

"Hell of scene we got here, huh?"

"Yeah, you could say that. You ever worked on something like this before?"

"Not quite, but close enough that I didn't need to throw up."

Hobbes could feel his face redden, and she patted him on the arm. "Hey, no judging. If I'd been the first to discover all this, I'd have horked up lunch from last Tuesday."

He laughed. "Thanks."

The tech nodded and left the scene. Hobbes sauntered over to the garden. Innocuous and ordinary, every garden store in the country probably sold the generic statue. But then, it wasn't the problem here. If Hobbes ever gambled, he would have bet the fish started talking to Marisa after she buried that first body under it.

He put his hand on the fish's tail. "Guilt does some crazy stuff to the head, doesn't it?"

Hobbes patted the koi twice then turned to walk away. A soft rustle, like a footstep moving through thick grass, echoed behind him. He spun around. Was the koi leaning a few inches more to the right?

He stepped backward, studying the statue, then scolded himself for being so jumpy. It came as no surprise, though, in the middle of this macabre scene. Hobbes smiled, but all he felt was cold.

He walked toward the gate. As he flipped the latch, the koi shifted, leaning more to the left. But Hobbes only moved forward, toward his car, and the mountain of paperwork awaiting him back at the office.

Madness is a divine release of the soul from the yoke of custom and convention. – Plato

GARDEN OF SECRETS

by R D Doan

Marisa finished pruning the roses and swept up the last of the mess before stepping back to admire her work. The small hidden garden at the Brinker Estate had been severely in need of tending after so many years of neglect. After hours of work, she had made it look as beautiful as the day she first laid eyes on it.

She sat against the wall on a stone bench and looked over her small garden with its white roses and statues. It was strange to think of it as anyone else's garden other than her Grandma Jo's; but she supposed it really was her garden now. After she signed the necessary paperwork, she had officially become the sole owner of the estate and all that lie on the grounds. The home had been kept up over the years by a maid service and the main garden was tended to regularly by a paid gardener, out of the estate funds of course, but the hidden garden had been left alone. It's inhabitants, the statues, were all but forgotten.

She almost hadn't come. She had sworn to herself years ago that she would never set foot in Kalamazoo again. Her father had tried to persuade her and had told her she owed it to her grandmother to honor her wishes. Grandma Jo had done so much for her by taking her in when she was young and he was away for work. She had even left her a scholarship fund that allowed her to go to USC in Los Angeles. However, it wasn't her father who had convinced her to come. She had her closest friends to thank instead. They wanted to go with her and make a trip of it. It would be the last trip they would have together as they were set to go their separate ways after they graduated. Marisa sat and talked to the statues, knowing they would make good listeners, and lamented the idea of being alone. She didn't want her friends to move on, for her life to change. The garden and its statues seemed to whisper back.

Marisa stood from the bench and pushed it to the side. She

used the blade of her pruning scissors to pry the stone paver block up and out of the ground that was just under the bench. She dug a few inches into the dirt and pulled out what she was looking for. She set the rectangular metal tin on the ground beside her, filled in the hole, and replaced the stone.

Sitting back on the bench, she opened the box and took out the antique Polaroid Land Camera that once belonged to Grandma Jo. It had been seven years since she last saw it. Touching it now sent chills down her spine. She put it back in the tin and closed the lid to gather her thoughts. Her friends were probably looking for her. She had left them at the main house while they looked around and she had been gone for quite a while. They had probably made their way to the main garden and would stumble upon her secret garden soon if she didn't get moving. The garden whispered and she stood to leave.

When Marisa emerged from the small gate hidden amongst the hedges, she was relieved to find the larger garden was empty. She walked among the rows of flowers, bushes and statues and slowly made her way back to the main house. As she made her way along the gravel path, memories of summers gone by began to flood her thoughts. She could hear her grandmother's voice singing while she gardened, and she saw a young Tommy Harrington running by in an apparent game of hide and seek. For a moment, she feared she were seeing ghosts, but soon realized they were only vivid memories; memories that weight heavily on her mind.

This place had a heaviness about it that made people feel uneasy. She too had been uneasy and a bit scared when she first came to the Brinker Estate as a child. Everything about the place had looked and felt off. There was, and still is, a heavy sadness that hangs in the air in the garden and to a lesser degree in the main house. Marisa often wondered if that blanket of sadness had been a result of the many tragedies her mother's family had endured, or if the sadness that was there was the root cause of all the tragedy.

She remembered her first impression of the Brinker Estate was that of a museum. When she thought of it now, she would have told her younger self that a mausoleum would have been a more accurate description. Despite the gloomy disposition and old decor, Marisa remembers that she was still awestruck by the beauty of the expansive garden that took up the whole of the property behind the main house. It was beautiful then, and it is just as breathtaking now, she thought.

She remembered the first thing Grandma Jo had ever spoken to her. She had been standing in the open doorway looking out onto the garden moments after arriving that first summer.

"You see that garden, Marisa?" Grandma Jo had asked. "She's been here for generations. For as long as anyone can remember, a Brinker has been here to tend to her and listen to her needs. Do you think you could help take care of her?"

"Yes, ma'am," Marisa had replied meekly.

"Good. Now, if you listen real hard, you'll hear her talk to ya. What's she asking for, Marisa?"

She remembers she could hear a faint mournful sobbing, but opted to say, "Nothing."

"You will. Someday, you will."

Marisa approached the back of the main house and saw her friends sitting on the steps to the back patio. They spotted her and came down to meet her. Emma practically ran.

"Oh my God, this place is awesome, girl!" she shrieked as she hugged Marisa.

"There are like, a million rooms in this place." Jessica gestured to the house behind her. "And this garden is sick! Why didn't you tell us about this place, Risa?"

Marisa shrugged. She looked at each of her friends and thought about their futures, about going their separate ways. She thought about what she could do to keep her friends together. She thought about what the garden had asked her.

"This place is like straight out of a movie or some shit," Emma said.

"And fancy as hell. Any idea why she left you the house and stuff? I mean, don't get me wrong, I'm super stoked for you, but, like, there must have been more people in her will, right?" Jessica asked.

"My mom was an only child, and Grandpa Brinker went missing when she was a kid. It was just Grandma Jo and my mom here for years, until my mom met my dad and moved to Traverse City. Grandma Jo was alone for a long time. Then, my mom ran off when I was seven and dad needed help raising me. He was a sailor on one of those Lake Freighters and couldn't take me with him, so he reached out to Grandma Jo and I stayed with her every summer until I was sixteen. Then she disappeared too."

For a moment, nobody said anything.

"I guess I was the only next of kin."

"You said she disappeared?" Emma asked.

"Yup," Marisa replied. Wanting to quickly change the subject, she said, "You guys want to order a pizza or something? I don't know about you, but I'm starving."

"I wonder why they're giving this place to you now?" Emma asked.

"I think you're declared dead after like seven years or something," replied Jessica.

Marisa had already started walking up to the house. Emma and Jessica followed, debating how many years it took to be missing before being declared deceased.

"You guys have got to try Erbelli's pizza. It's to die for." Marisa said as they went in the back door to the kitchen.

The breeze outside blew, and the garden whispered in agreement.

That evening, they ate pizza, drank wine, and talked about USC, boys, and their new jobs that start in a few months. As the empty wine bottles started to pile up, their conversations turned to Marisa's past, her family, and of course, the Brinker Estate. Marisa didn't have much more to offer them as she didn't really know much about the history of the estate herself. She told them that Grandma Jo didn't really talk too much about it. All she ever said was there was always a Brinker living there and the property had been in the family for generations.

Jessica mused on the age of the estate and asked if either Emma or Marisa thought it was haunted.

"I think all old houses are haunted, and this house is old as shit. You see any ghosts here when you stayed here Risa?" Emma asked.

Marisa thought for a moment before answering, "No. I don't

think I've seen any ghosts. But…"

"But what?" Jessica replied, after nearly choking on her wine.

"Look, I don't really believe in ghosts. Well, not in the sense that there are spirits roaming around the halls at night and stuff." Marisa took another gulp of wine before going on. "Do I think the place is haunted? Sure, I do. Not by ghost though, by memories. What if, instead of ghosts being spirits of the dead that are trapped here on earth, they're actually memories that happened here that are imprinted on this place forever. Like a photo. And the house, or garden, or whatever, is the photo album. We don't see the ghost of the dead, but we see the memory instead."

"That's deep, girl," Emma remarked.

"To memories," Jessica toasted, raising her nearly empty glass of wine.

"To memories!" Marisa and Emma cheered.

The girls decided to get some fresh air and check out the garden under the lights. Marisa had mentioned that the garden was beautiful at night when she was younger, with hanging lights and solar lights along the paths. That night, it was just as she remembered.

Jessica grabbed another glass of wine, Marisa grabbed her handbag, and they strolled along the garden paths, admiring the statues in the garden. Jessica was getting a little tipsy and Marisa feared she might break something or puke somewhere in the garden. Emma didn't seem to be bothered by the wine at all. Marisa wasn't surprised. She thought Em had graduated to an alcoholic before she graduated from USC.

They stopped in front of a statue of a teenage boy and Marisa's heart fell to her stomach. She could hear a faint whisper in the breeze. She avoided the stone boy's eyes, afraid of what might look back.

"Dis one's a handsome one, hey Em?" Jessica slurred, while she caressed the biceps of the boy's outstretched arm.

"Yeah, a real fuckin charmer too. What kinda flower is that he's holding Risa?" Emma asked.

"A daisy," Marisa replied at almost a whisper. "A daisy," she repeated, louder. "This is a statue of Thomas Harrington. He was my first crush."

"I see why," Jessica said as she stroked his biceps.

"You know he ain't real, Jes. Right? It's a fucking statue." Emma replied.

Marisa's thoughts drifted to the last night she saw Thomas. Grandma Jo had invited Thomas to dinner and Marisa had been over the moon. After dinner, they had strolled through the garden together and he picked her a daisy, her favorite flower. He had asked her to cover her eyes, as to surprise her with the flower. She had heard the sound of a camera shutter, and confused, she opened her eyes. She screamed in horror when she found the love of her life frozen in stone before her, his flower to her still in his hands.

"Earth to Risa!" Emma was snapping her fingers in front of Marisa's face. "Hey girl, where'd you go off to?"

"What? Oh, sorry. I guess… I guess I was just thinking of when we got this statue."

"We were asking you why you got a statue of your old crush in the family garden," Emma said.

"Grandma Jo said she had it made so I wouldn't ever have to let him go. She said if I had a statue of him, I could always be with him. It would keep his memory alive and here forever."

"That's silly," slurred Jessica.

"I'm with the drunk. That's bullshit. But, props to granny for caring about your feelings," Emma said while trying to pry Jessica away from the statue's arm.

Marisa dared a look at Thomas' eyes and saw a single tear on the statue's right cheek. Her heart broke all over again.

They were walking along the back hedge now, and Jessica was arguing with Emma about her ability to walk. She swore up and down that Emma was making it worse, and she could "Do it myself!"

Emma let go, and Jessica took two wobbly steps on her own before promptly falling sideways into the hedge.

"I told you, girl! You're too drunk to walk by yourself."

"Hey you guys! There's a little metal gate back here!" Jessica cried out from in the hedge.

Marisa closed her eyes and took a steadying breath and listened to the whispering in the air. "Yeah, I know. You guys wanna see my secret garden?"

When they entered the small ten-foot square garden, hidden behind tall hedges along the back of the property, the girls were awestruck. It would be hard not to. The work Marisa had done earlier that day to spruce up the garden had paid off. The white roses everywhere were beautiful. The garden was illuminated with strings of hanging light bulbs that gave the quaint garden a homey feel. The statues were placed so as to give the impression they were welcoming them to the garden. Their eyes seemed to look right at them.

Emma put Jessica on the bench against the wall and walked slowly up to the statues.

"Who are these statues of?" she asked.

"The man over there is my grandfather Brinker. The woman reaching out to the rose bush is my mother."

"Is this older woman your Grandma Jo?" Emma asked, looking a little confused.

"Actually, yes. Yes, it is."

"Why is she on her knees in prayer?"

"She's not praying. She's pleading."

"What?"

"Why don't you sit down next to Jes and I'll tell you about this garden." Marisa gestured to the bench where Jessica was napping now.

Emma nudged Jessica and prompted her to sit up. She sat down and Jessica leaned on her shoulder and started to sleep again.

"The is my Grandma Jo's secret garden. I found it the night she turned Thomas into a statue."

"What do you mean she turned him into a," Emma started.

"Don't interrupt. Let me just get this out. It's hard enough as it is. Just listen."

Emma nodded.

"I was terrified, horrified. I didn't know what to do, or where to go, so I ran. I saw a thin part in the hedge and leapt in to hide. I found the gate, just like Jes did tonight. I came here to hide, but she came in after me. It was here that I learned the horrible truth. I saw the statue of my mother and I knew then what had happed. Grandma Jo had gotten to her and turned her to stone. She said she did it to keep her here. So she couldn't run away again. I'm pretty sure she did the same to Grandpa Brinker too. Don't you see? They never really left. They're still here!"

"But," Emma hesitated. Her voice cracked with fear as she spoke. "But why is your Grandma Jo pleading, Risa?"

"Because," Marisa's face darkened and began to crack a sly smile. "She heard what I heard when the garden spoke that night."

Emma began to cry as Marisa walked slowly toward the bench.

Marisa pulled out the Polaroid Land Camera from her handbag and started to get it ready.

"The garden whispered to me that she turned them to stone with the camera. She had set the camera down on that very bench when she attempted to comfort me. She told me she did what she did to keep the ones we love with us forever. I was mad, Em. I was scared and angry with her. So, I got up and grabbed the camera. I aimed it at her. She kneeled and pleaded with me to reconsider. We both heard the garden speak then. She pleaded and I snapped the picture."

"What... What did the garden say?" Emma asked in a small shaking voice.

"Take the shot, Marisa. A picture here will last forever," she said.

She snapped the photo. The garden whispers were right. Her friends would never leave her now. They would sit here forever and always be here for her.

UNNERVED

by Max Carrey

Knuckles rasp upon the door and Marisa jumps dropping the ladle into the pot with a big clanging splash. Scuttling to the door, the bloated wood from the heavy rain cause a strange muffled creak to sound as it's heaved open. A man wearing a widely brimmed hat with a plastic covering, tan pants, and a brownish green jacket with a shiny star badge pinned to it stands before her.

"Can I help you Sir?"

"I'm Sheriff Kim, Mam. If I could come in a moment and have a word with you I'd be much obliged."

"Yes, yes, please…" she mutters jovially ushering him inside. "It is absolutely horrendous outside!"

Sheriff Kim hustles himself in, as Marisa fights against the wind to close the door. He remains motionless beside the entrance to her little cabin, clutching himself.

"Please, come by the fire and warm yourself Sheriff Kim."

"Oh, I wouldn't want to muddy your lovely floors Mam."

"You're no bother really, come in, come in and make yourself at home," she waves him on to follow.

His dark scrutinizing eyes wash over everything, easily enough too, as the whole of the cabin is contained in one massive space with a tiny offshoot for a bed and bath. The lighting is dimmed, soft against such a harsh and stormy night. Though it is warm, welcoming, tidy, and an intoxicating smell of chicken broth is bubbling away on the stove.

He follows, unfurling his curled shoulders, rain droplets shed down him in a sheet of mimicked rain, but Marisa doesn't seem to mind and leads him to sit down upon the couch opposite of her chair.

A wisp of cool breath brushes past the nape of his neck, and he swivels around in his seat, finding no one there. Shaking his head he positions himself back to face her, although a bit on edge.

"So what is it that you would like to discuss?" she asks as she gently folds her hands down upon her lap, and he notes crusty white plaster tipping her fingers.

"I wanted to inform you of the disappearances-"

Her smile drops off her face, "Disappearances?"

"Yes Mam-"

"Marisa, Marisa Davenport if you please."

"Miss Davenport as you might already be aware there was a hiker that went missing two weeks ago-"

Air licks at his neck again, and he slaps a hand there, rubbing it.

"Did you find him?"

"No."

"How terrible," her voice trembles, and her brow furrows up in worry, catching the shadows cast by the fire.

"We can't be sure whether or not he's lost or perhaps he simply wanted to disappear from his life without a trace."

"I see...how strange..." her voice trails off and dies in the air. She inhales sharply. "But you don't think that's the case?"

"Yesterday a biker was reported missing in these woods."

"It could be a coincidence, or maybe..." her face is screwed up in thought, but she snaps herself out of it. "I'm sorry. I read too many mystery novels."

Sheriff Kim cracks a smile. "Quite alright Miss Davenport, can't say that mystery novels didn't put the interest in me to become a sheriff." He sniffles away the cold as icy air tickles his nose. "Someone's taken them or, forgive my lack of tactfulness, murdered them."

"You-you really think so?" she asks breathlessly, a slight chill shivers over her despite how close she sits to the fire.

"I do," he replies firmly. "There's just something... strange about it all, something doesn't sit right with me," he pauses to shake his head, as if contemplating the validity of his own mind, "And when I heard of you out here all by yourself I thought it would be best to come and check on you, inform you, so you can stay aware and stay safe."

A grin pushes up her rosy cheeks, though her skin has turned a sickly yellow from the light. "How awfully kind of you Sheriff," she says, widening her smile.

Something thumps in the little offshoot bedroom, but his eyes catch sight of nothing and Miss Davenport has remained still and unresponsive to the noise.

"But I also came to ask you questions… Do you know anything? Seen anyone out here? Heard anything?" He learns forward in his seat, eyes squinted in interrogation.

A lazy *thump* sounds in the kitchen, though his eyes see the pot on the stove sputtering away and it calms his aggravated nerves.

"No, no…it's so quiet out here, at least in this part of the woods," she chuckles, "and I'm not prone to receiving visitors."

"What is it you do out here, if you don't mind me asking? I'm rather new to the area and I'm afraid I have overlooked coming to introduce myself to you."

"Oh, no worries Sheriff," she waves it off without a care, "it is also my fault; for you see I prefer to keep to myself. I'm an artist, a sculptor. The quiet of the woods helps to keep me focused."

His eyes relax somewhat, and a grin cracks his own façade. "Ah, that would explain the hands."

"What?" She looks down and finds plaster coating her fingertips, and begins to rub them furiously against her apron, but it's too well dried to budge except for miniscule crumbly bits dusting the floor. Her voice staggers, "Oh my, I'm getting quite clumsy."

"Usually quite tidy are you?" He cocks an eyebrow. "I'm ashamed to say I'm horrifically messy myself."

She flashes a more timid smile before letting loose a giggle that suffocates against the tense warm air. "Yes, I pride myself on it…although I can't say that I do right now."

A subtle splash and Kim's eyes catch the ripple in the water before it fades, pointing to the puddle he created on the floor he voices warily, "I suppose I helped contribute to that."

"No, no…messes are good."

"Really?"

His eyes turn wild.

"Of course, if there weren't any messes there'd be nothing to clean up," she declares jovially. Her young smooth pretty young face, so carefree and innocent.

Sheriff Kim swivels in his seat uncomfortably.

"Was that your work outside?"

"Oh yes, yes," she exclaims jumping up, striding across the room in a couple of bounds. "These are just some of my creations, the ones that I've decided to keep."

Sheriff Kim thoroughly warmed through, leaves the fire to go stand by Miss Davenport. She is holding open the curtains, gazing down upon her garden.

His eyes shift to the delicately made statues, surprising due to their plaster and cement makeup, but it's the way the lines of their body and face are so accurately carved that you can make out every muscle or lump of fat...an array of bodies on full display.

A rather short woman with arms stretched out to beckon people toward the cabin. A tall man reaching up in a tree, for an apple he'll never get. A man lying prone on the grass with his head cradled in his hands staring up at the stars. And a woman, lean and athletic, in mid run up on her podium.

"You're-" the floor creaks behind him, snapping his attention back. The firelight flickers, licking in odd waves.

"Don't be startled Sheriff. This is an old cabin, it yawns from time to time."

He feigns a smile, and directing his gaze back to her statues finishes his thought, "You're immensely talented."

"Thank you, thank you... You know, I could make you a garden statue, if you wished."

Footsteps scrape the floors behind him, but when he whips around to look no one else is there.

"I'm afraid it makes more noise during storms," she says, taking note of his jumpiness.

Just then the storm picks up outside, rain beating so hard against the roof it reverberates like hail. Sheriff Kim relaxes somewhat, but his shoulders are still squared tensely.

"What is that?" he asks, his finger pressed against the glass pointing down below to the little cedar building with blacked out windows.

"Oh, my shed? I use it as my work shop."

He nods, dropping his finger from the glass.

"Do you want to see inside? I mean, I don't usually because it's quite messy and I prefer people to not see works in progress...gives the wrong impression."

"Oh, no...no I understand. Forgive my curiosity."

"Not at all," she smiles kindly, "perhaps another day when the weather is better and it is not so late."

"I do apologize for coming by at such a late-"

A throaty exhale wisps through the air, catching Sheriff Kim's ears. He jolts and then shivers, his eyes darting about wildly, looking for the source.

"Sheriff? Are you alright?" she asks, her gaze trying to follow his about her cabin, before coming to rest upon his pale face. "You look as if you are hearing ghosts."

He twitches and his fingers flex. Words stumbling out his agape mouth, "Do you ever hear them...Miss Davenport?"

She lulls her head to the side, and stares off in thought. "I suppose sometimes, at certain hours when one is more inclined for such things. It can be quite lonely out here."

"I can only imagine," he says, pulling in his still slick jacket around him, "but you must really love your work then."

"I do," her eyes flick back to his, and the smile reappears, "that I do."

Another creak of the floorboards and Sheriff Kim rolls his shoulders unnervingly.

"Well, thank you for your hospitality."

Marisa's face drops, her blue eyes drowning in themselves. "Oh my," she throws a hand up in front of her mouth in shock, "I'm afraid I've been a terrible host! I didn't offer you anything to drink."

"It is quite alright Miss Davenport," he breathlessly remarks.

"Marisa, please."

"Marisa," he corrects while attempting a smile, yet his eyes continue to dart about with each new fleeting sound. "Thank you for your time."

"My pleasure, stop by anytime… " She trails him to the door, and upon opening it the rain shoots in at an angle, wind blustering through to thrash at the curtains, and Sheriff Kim braces himself to reenter the storm. Yet, before he goes Marisa stops him with her curiosity rising above the thundering noise, "Oh but Sheriff, do you mind my asking…what it is?"

"What is what Marisa?"

She pauses a moment, eyelashes flicking away the misty rain, studying his face. Her delicate lips part and she says, "The thing that doesn't sit right with you."

"Oh…," he pauses, thinking back to earlier when he'd mentioned the disappearances, and his gaze travels along every seam between the hardwood floor, every line of her countertop, the grout along the backsplash, the dustless and polished furniture, and every elegantly fluffed pillow of hers. "It's all too clean, as if they vanished into thin air."

The edges of her mouth sink, pulling downward, her tone low and vibrating, "How frightening."

"Yes, yes…well, goodnight," he says with a hesitancy that is palpable, taking one last look about the cabin before stepping off into the dark torrential night.

"Goodnight," she calls out to him, before closing the door.

Striding over to the window, she pulls back the curtains to peek through, watching the Sheriff maneuver his slopping boots through her garden, eyeing her statues as he goes. The lean athletic woman, the dreamy man gazing upward, the man in constant reach of an apple and the woman trying to usher him back in, yet he disappears.

The floorboards creak behind her and she whips around snapping, "Would you be quiet!"

The air is empty but she doesn't relent glaring it down, until her eyes break to note the mess. All the rain upon the floor, the boot prints, the rustled curtains, the overdone broth splattering the stove. Her fingers itch to clean it all up, make it spotless again, but her mind wants more chaos. To break it all down and build it back up is the chance to make it better than before.

A dash of inspiration streaks through her, creating a picture she must mold to match.

Grabbing her raincoat she braves the weather, weaving circles around her mud splattered pieces of art until alighting to her workshop. The sky thunders and cracks overhead, but it doesn't hinder the screams she can hear echo among the silence.

Stepping inside, locking herself in, the little shed goes completely quiet as if no storm rages. Soundproofing spills from the walls, as do all her tools. Her plaster, her cement and other compounds, her chisel, her carving knives, and vast array of clamps surround the workbench. Her latest piece is splayed out upon the table. She rasps her knuckles against it finding it set, dried to perfection but rough around the edges.

Originally it was going to be a much simpler piece, yet her mind has transfixed upon a new idea, and it causes her to manically smile, her nerves tingle with delight.

She releases the clamps that have pinned down her creation's elbows, and locked her knees in place. Grinding suctioned pops crack against the silence, and a whimpering cry slinks in Marisa's ears trying to bury itself there, but she ignores it.

She trails a finger across the smooth wash of surface that should be her statue's lips, but the tape underneath has made it a crude representation. She twists and twirls her fingers above it, as she imagines how to sculpt the likeness back into it...the life back into it.

Footsteps pitter patter behind her, breathy cries flick across her skin, the echoes of pain and whimpering pleas still pulsate in the air. *They* never truly leave... and now they only manage to stir the vigor within her further.

"You will be my Venus de Milo," she whispers to her creation.

Reaching to a shelf she draws up a hatchet, the sharp edge shining in the light, she then swiftly brings it down right at the left shoulder.

CRACK!

She braces her foot against the workbench as she heaves the blade free, but then brings it down a final time.

One last deafening crack, and the blade sinks down into the wood of the workbench. Pulling it away the arm breaks free, separating from the rest of the body, plaster shattering onto the floor.

Marisa leans down to inspect her work, her smile widening, eyes glinting with anticipation.

"You're going to be so beautiful."

The cut has revealed the meaty fleshy core of the piece. The thin layer of skin underneath the plaster, the coagulated blood inside shriveling veins, coarse muscle, and splintered bone... it's all messy now, but it will be cleaned up and perfect soon.

She stands straight, stretching her back until her spine pops. Her fingers tighten against the hatchet, as her voice low and threatening hisses into the night, "Now onto the other arm!"

MARISA'S CURSE

by Clark Roberts

Whack!
Despite the white ball's initial straight line flight, Joyce's husband elicited a grunt beneath his breath.
"Hold on," Charlie said from the tee box. He looked like a still-shot, statuesque, in his swing's follow-through.
The ball sailed into the blue sky, an obvious bend taking shape in its trajectory.
"Hold Ooooon!" Charlie urged through clenched teeth. He leaned in the opposite direction the ball sliced.
In the golf cart, Joyce set her phone down and smiled at her husband's childish effort to alter the shot through mental will—nothing mean spirited, she just got a kick seeing how serious he could take this game.
"Awww hell," Charlie spat.
Two hundred yards up where the thirteenth hole dog-legged left, the ball flew straight into the trees, followed by the sound of it striking solid wood.
Crows scattered into flight, and that was all Joyce could handle.
Despite covering her mouth with the back of her hand she couldn't stifle the laughter, and once the first chuckle barked out it was as impossible to stop as an errant golf shot.
"Oh, shut up," Charlie said. He tried glowering at his wife, but a grin broke over his face. His shoulders hung a little too much as he slumped back to the cart, and he slammed his driver down into the golf bag with a little too much force. When he sat behind the wheel and next to Joyce the smile had grown. He stared straight down the fairway and lamented, "So much for the perfect round."
Joyce studied her husband's face—the late summer golden tan that came to him so naturally each year, the silver hair he refused to dye poking out from the visor specifically reserved for golf, the etched crow's feet at his eyes and the deep laugh lines only sixty

odd years of good living could produce. Almost hushed, she said, "I love you, Charlie."

"Me too," he said. He reached and tenderly placed a hand on her bare knee. "I never could have asked for a better wife."

Joyce watched as her husband's chest proudly filled with air. He leaned over and they kissed. After forty years of being together, moments like these were often quick, often few and far between, but they were a blessing.

Most importantly, in her heart Joyce knew these moments were authentic between them.

Charlie pressed the gas pedal and the golf cart took off smoothly.

"*Marisa's Curse* is the one that gets me every time," Charlie said. Now in the rough, the cart lightly bounced alongside the fairway down to the dog-leg.

As they drove forward, Joyce went back to the internet connection on her phone.

"What's *Marisa's Curse*?" she asked, truly perplexed.

"It's what they call lucky thirteen."

"Strange name for a golf hole." She knew they all had titles—mostly nature related, cute plays like *Call of the Loons, The Stream's Revenge* and even the romantic *Love in the Pines.* "What's *Marisa's Curse* reference?"

"Research it on your phone," Charlie said. "You spend more time on that than cheering me on."

"I think I will," Joyce answered with obvious faux smugness.

"Be prepared. It's a disturbing tale."

They jounced along in the rough while Joyce continued studying her phone. The farther she scrolled down and read, the more and more twisted the hole's history sounded.

Charlie guided the cart near the edge of the woods. As they transitioned from sunlight into the shade, a shiver overtook Joyce.

She couldn't fathom what she was researching.

"Is this true?" she asked.

Charlie stopped the cart where his ball had entered. He shrugged as he rocked out of the cart. "I'm sure it's at least a half-truth. Not a pleasant tale, that's for certain." He assessed the foliage through which he'd have to fight. "Sheesh, looks like I should've brought along a machete."

Joyce quickly reread the disturbing history.

"A beautiful and challenging par five, Marisa's Curse is quite possibly the most infamous golf hole in northern Michigan. Its history is steeped in dark lore.

In the early 1900s before being developed into the beautiful course that is Dragon's Run, the previous landowners had a curious daughter. In her eighth year, young Marisa set out to explore the surrounding woods without her parents' permission. She became lost, and despite the organization of search parties that spanned four full days, the girl was not retrieved. Weeks later, dirty and starving and pale, she returned home on her own, seemingly out of the blue. Young Marisa was never quite the same. She spent days at a time nearly catatonic, and whenever she did speak it was of a mystical dragon she claimed to have met in the woods during her time spent lost to the world. One day, Marisa again went missing. When search parties organized this time, they were not so lucky as to come back empty handed. She was found dead, burned to a crisp near the current location of hole thirteen's dog-leg. Newspapers from the era report smoke was still curling from the body when the yelling father walked up on his pride and joy.

Legend has it that the land near the dog-leg is now cursed. That every so often an unfortunate golfer searching for a lost ball will stumble upon a stone representation of a dragon, a little garden statue that has no earthly business being in these woods. That man is then cursed to soon meet his demise. Even worse, his golf game will never recover.

The authenticity of the tale is up for debate. Yet one thing is agreed upon unanimously; the curse has passed a shiver down many a golfer's backs after an errant tee shot off Marisa's Curse."

"This is terrible," Joyce exclaimed to no one in particular. She tossed her phone into the cart's cubby. "Charlie, maybe you should take a penalty stroke and drop a ba…"

She paused. Only trees and ferns and brush stared back at her.

"Charlie…" she called.

A hole or two over, a group of men celebrated what must have been a fine putt, their voices muted by the woods.

Joyce cautiously stepped from the cart. She could barely see through the dense foliage at the edge of the woods. Why anyone thought they could even line a shot up through this mess was beyond her.

But that's not what really bothered her.

There was a vibe coming from the forest, something unsettling, something wrong.

Stop scaring yourself, she thought. *The story was probably dreamed up by the owners to draw customers.*

From deeper in the woods, a god-awful moan.

It was without doubt Charlie, and he sounded more terrified than Joyce could ever imagine.

"Charlie!" she yelled.

Again the moan, and even though an icy whisper at the back of her mind warned her not to move forward, she pushed through the threshold and entered the woods.

Once inside and past the brush line, the forest floor opened up immediately. Withered leaves covered the ground and crunched beneath each step Joyce took.

To her left, Joyce heard her husband sob. Twenty feet up she saw the bright orange of his golf shirt.

His back was to her and his head bowed.

Slowly, she approached. Before she reached a distance where she could touch his shoulder, Charlie turned.

Tears streamed down his cheeks.

"Charlie, what's wrong?"

"I saw something."

The red in his eyes signaled a childlike terror of being forever forgotten by the world.

Joyce waited for more, making no remark. She'd only seen her husband cry three times—at both of his parents' funerals and then when giving away their daughter on her wedding day—here was the fourth, and it was entirely different.

"Jesus wept," Charlie sobbed, "I saw the dragon."

Joyce closed her mouth and breathed through her nose.

"Right here," Charlie continued. He turned back and with his three iron lightly tapped the ground. "It was right here."

Joyce could see nothing but parchment-like leaves littering the ground. She remained mute.

"It was here, damnit! RIGHT HERE!" Charlie pounded the club head into the ground before wheeling back on Joyce. Sheer desperation flamed to his face. "The stone statue of the dragon was with me. I swear I'm telling you the truth."

Because there was nothing else to say, she replied, "I believe you."

She wanted to go to him, offer a hug, but also was afraid to move any closer to where Charlie had indicated. A sense of impropriety effused from the spot.

Then Charlie was crying again, and it was the saddest and most desperate filled moment Joyce had ever witnessed in her sixty-four years of life.

She whispered, "I think we should leave the woods, Charlie."

When he stepped abreast of her, Joyce placed one gentle hand at his back and the other at his bicep—guiding him like one might lead a lost child to the front of a store.

They exited the woods without speaking.

Charlie sniffled to regain his composure. Wiping away tears, he started up the cart and sped past the thirteenth putting green without a glance.

At fourteen's tee box—aptly titled *The Dragon's Pool* for the shimmering pond along the putting green's edge—Charlie dug a new ball out of his bag. He waggled his club and stroked a shot that split the fairway.

But nothing else went right for him the rest of the round, because only eighty yards out from hole fourteen's flag, peripherally aware of the pond, he skulled the second shot and sent the ball flying past the green. He flubbed the next chip shot, and ended up writing in a triple-bogey on the scorecard for what was considered the one of the easiest par fours of the course.

He bogied fifteen and sixteen, and on seventeen he sailed another drive deep into the woods.

For her part, Joyce mostly stared at her shoes, unsure for the first time in ages of how to comfort the man she loved, because what was occurring had nothing to do with his golf swing. She sensed that something had…

…*changed*…

inside Charlie.

The cart rolled to a stop near where his last drive had flown.

Joyce watched as he pulled a club from his bag and approached the wood line.

Was he really going back into the trees?

A wind picked up out of nowhere, and Charlie halted right at the edge, one foot paused in mid air.

He suddenly doubled over and puked. When he straightened back up, his face was the color of off-white candle wax. He made his way back to the cart, sat with both hands gripping the black steering wheel. He stared vacantly at the score card.

He whispered, "I saw *Marisa's Curse* on thirteen. I'm done for the day."

That night, Joyce dreamed of trying to save a man from a pool of quicksand. She was deep in a jungle, and minimal sunlight filtered through the canopy. Only a length of arm jutted up, waving desperately from the center of the pool. Joyce leaned forward and the hand latched onto her forearm. She pulled with all her might and there was some give from the quicksand. Next, a great shadow draped over her and chilled Joyce. She turned and glanced over her shoulder. A giant dragon loomed—all scales, fangs, and smoking nostrils. There was a great sucking sound as the quicksand seemed to re-strengthen and pulled down with a force far beyond what Joyce could manage. She let go, and the hand disappeared, fingers taut and splayed desperately. Before the hand was completely swallowed, her stare intensified tenfold and she recognized the gold wedding band with the three diamond studs outlining the top.

Joyce startled awake into an upright position. She breathed heavily.

Charlie's side of the bed was empty. She quickly scanned the bedroom and realized she was alone. Her heart trip-hammered against her chest.

She thought to herself, *you're too weak for these kinds of frights, ole girl.* And then, *Charlie just went to the bathroom.*

A second voice, one that emitted from a colder, arctic region of the brain whispered, *oh no, Deary, he certainly is not simply using the potty.*

The unbidden vision of the dragon from her shattered dream rose in her mind.

She swung her feet out of bed. When she touched down on the carpeting, a familiar sound reverberated throughout the house— the garage door rattling in its tracks.

Truly startled, Joyce went to the garage as fast as her old legs would carry her.

Here was Charlie, dressed in his bathrobe and leaning against his Lexus for support. He stared off into darkness.

The air breathing into the garage from the night was chilly, and Joyce pulled her own bathrobe tighter. Unlike earlier at the golf course, she was able to approach Charlie.

"Come back to bed," she said at his side.

"She was trapped in here," Charlie answered. The glazed look of earlier once again dulled his eyes. "Her crying woke me up and led me out here."

"Who?" Deep in Joyce's guts where things really counted, the answer was already there like an open gravesite awaiting a burial.

"The lost girl—Marisa. She was crying and saying she wanted to go home, so I opened the garage door for her."

"Oh Charlie, please, *please* tell me this is all one of your jokes."

He locked eyes with Joyce as firmly as the day they'd committed their wedding vows. He shook his head, "No joke. She left, but I think I'm supposed to go with her. She asked me to follow her."

Joyce licked her lips. In her soothing voice, she said, "You'll do no such thing. You need to come back to bed with me."

They did go back to bed.

Charlie was asleep in minutes.

Joyce, fretting over her husband's mental state, tossed and turned until the first slip of sun shone through their bedroom window.

League night rolled around later in the week.

"I don't like it," Joyce said. She sat at the small card table Charlie had hauled out of the back room for her. Puzzle pieces splayed out before her, and she nearly had all of the sides completed and then it was just a matter of letting the middle pieces fall into place.

"I have to play," Charlie insisted. "Ted is counting on me."

"He could always call on a reserve for one night," Joyce suggested. She plucked up the last corner piece and firmly snapped it in place.

"Ted and I are sitting comfortably in third," Charlie explained. He rattled the ice in the tumbler glass he held, and poured another—one of his fine whiskeys on the rocks. "We're up against team Bob and Carl this afternoon, and those guys are in second.

We take this match tonight and then there's just one rider ahead to chase down." Charlie winked.

"I'm concerned." Joyce neatly placed both hands down on the table, palms down. "What happened with you was strange—scary even. And do you really think you need another drink if you're driving?"

"You're probably right." Charlie assessed the whiskey. He splashed what he'd just poured into the kitchen sink. "Look, I know what happened was... *odd*. At this point, it's almost like a dream to me, because I've felt better the past couple days. I think the sun got to me."

"It was hardly a scorcher on Monday, and it most definitely wasn't a dream."

"I can't let Ted down. There's no way around it, I've got to play tonight."

"But that dreadful story—*Marisa's Curse* or whatever. I don't like it one bit."

Then Charlie was at Joyce's side and hunched down to her level. He kissed her cheek. Gently, he patted her hand. "I'll be fine tonight. I promise."

Joyce pressed her lips, stared at the puzzle.

Charlie offered a smile, and then he was in the back room rummaging up his golf clubs. In a matter of minutes he was out the door.

Joyce was close to halfway finished with the jigsaw puzzle—had almost completely convinced herself that everything would be fine with Charlie, that the entire out of the universe experience had been nothing more than a strange anomaly—her cell phone dinged an incoming message from Ted Bentley.

"There's been an incident. I'm driving Charlie home. You'll have to make arrangements for his car or get it in the morning."

Joyce, her one hand up to trembling lips, read over the message more than a couple times. Inside her chest, it felt as if her heart was ripping in half.

One good thing about the message was that Charlie was coming home, so an ambulance hadn't been called.

Joyce typed out a return question: *"What happened?"*

Ted: *"An incident. It's too difficult to explain through texts. I'll drop him off shortly."*

When Ted pulled into the drive, Joyce had the door open so he could immediately walk his partner inside.

It was obvious from the stumbling steps that Charlie needed the help. He collapsed on the sofa, breathing in deep gasps. Sweat gleaned from his brow.

"He's drunk," Ted said matter-of-factly, beating Joyce to her question.

"But he never has too many on league night," Joyce said.

"I know," Ted agreed. "In our twenty years as partners I've never witnessed Charlie put 'em down like he did tonight. We're in the last stretch of the league so each night is a full round of eighteen. He must have had four beers on the front nine and then double-fisted two whiskey and cokes at the turn."

"Didn't you tell him to cool it?"

"I'm sorry Joyce, but I did," Ted nodded. "But he was a man on a mission. Can't say that I'm too pleased about it. This was a big match for us tonight, and then he goes and passes out at the tee on thirteen."

Joyce's world swirled—*passed out at thirteen*—and even though Ted went on to explain with fuller details his voice was zoned out by her.

"Thank you, Ted," she said almost absently. "I'll handle it from here."

"Just know none of this is my fault, and Charlie let me down too."

With more sharpness Joyce repeated, "I said *thank you.*"

"Alright then." Ted nodded. He showed himself to the door.

In the kitchen, Joyce drew a glass of water from the tap. She went back and sat next to Charlie, held the glass to his lips.

He sipped laboriously, was thrown into a coughing fit, and on a second effort was able to swallow the water. The fresh water seemed to do the trick, and he sat up straighter.

"She was waiting for me," Charlie spoke.

There was no reason to ask about whom he was speaking, so Joyce stayed quiet.

"Right in the middle of thirteen's fairway. I went to draw my backswing, and I peeked up like I always do. She was right there staring at me. Nobody else saw her, but she was there. Even from a distance I could feel her Joyce, *feel* her boring straight into my soul."

Joyce put the glass back to his lips and it tapped against his teeth.

Charlie drank, and with closed eyes said, "She haunts me."

Another nightmare afflicted Joyce that night. This time she was fleeing through a forest while holding hands with Charlie. Something so large it shook the ground chased after them. Joyce heard tree trunks snapping like twigs. Sprint as they might, she and Charlie were old and were no match for the hunting goliath behind them. Like in the dream nights earlier, Joyce glanced over her shoulder and sure enough—the scales, the monstrous head, the gold rimmed eyes filled with malice. This time, the dragon opened its mouth, and a pond sized ball of fire shot forth. The heat was excruciating, and Joyce felt not only her skin melting away but also her bones.

She blinked awake, curled in the fetal position and clutching Charlie's pillow to her bosom.

The bedroom door had been left wide. Joyce heard the refrigerator hum to life from the other section of the house.

She searched the room with her eyes.

The same as Monday night, no Charlie.

She went to investigate and this time discovered the garage door had already been opened. Without Charlie's car parked inside the garage, it seemed full of nothing but space. Charlie was nowhere to be seen. Only the pitch dark of night stared back at Joyce.

She did notice one thing peculiar. Charlie's bike, the sleek futuristic thing he'd bought when he'd for a few years caught an interest in triathlons, was missing.

You know where he's gone to.

Joyce rushed back inside, grabbed her own car keys and a flashlight. In her haste to leave, she forgot her cell phone.

It was only once she was on the road that her mind groped for an explanation as to why she wasn't alerting the authorities. Although none came to her—beyond a feeling of fate—she continued to drive out to *Dragon's Run*.

The roads were empty this time of night. She searched the sides for any sign of Charlie.

Being well past midnight by the time she wheeled into *Dragon's Run*, the parking lot was empty save for Charlie's Lexus parked in the rear corner. There, she also discovered his discarded bike.

Outside her car, Joyce flicked the flashlight to life. She forced courage into her nerves and followed the sharp beam.

With the tall trees standing sentry at each fairway's edge and blocking out most of the moonlight, the land was beyond dark.

The fear inside was real and hastened her steps.

She hustled down eighteen's fairway, turned left to pass seventeen's putting green. Halfway down seventeen she cut over through the woods taking the shortest route to thirteen—*Marisa's Curse*.

When she stepped onto thirteen's fairway, her feet froze.

A shadow waited for her at the opposite tree line. As dark as it was, Joyce could still make out the figure was small enough to be a young girl.

Just when Joyce had convinced herself it was her mind playing a trick, the girl's arm shot up and waved, calling Joyce to the other side. The girl turned and pushed through the brush at thirteen's dog-leg.

Joyce scampered across the fairway, the beam of light bouncing erratically. There was no hesitation at the wood line, she broke though with considerable ease as if the forest here had invited her as a guest.

Something like burnt barbecue immediately assaulted her nostrils. In a panic, Joyce swung the light to and fro but found no little girl.

She did, however, discover a body—charred black and the flesh still smoking.

Wanting it to not be true, she studied the body. From the black as ash left hand there was a glitter against the light.

Joyce didn't need to inspect the gold ring any closer to know three diamonds studded the top of the wedding band.

"Why?" she asked the night. "Why did you come back here, Charlie?"

The dry leaves behind her rustled, as if answering.

She swung the light.

Not more than a child's jump away, a stone garden statue stared up at her. Smoke curled heavenward from the carved nostrils.

A hand of ice so cold it actually burned seemed to squeeze Joyce's heart.

Her blood froze. She fell backwards. Her back smacked the ground next to her husband.

The flashlight rolled from her hand.

When the third group of golfers made the grisly discovery the following morning, the flashlight's batteries were dead.

MARISA'S STATUE

by Radar DeBoard

    Ada looked down at the familiar stepping stones she had seen before. The multiple colors swirled together into a unique pinwheel pattern. With hesitant steps she moved forward slowly through the well-trimmed hedges that surrounded her. Once she noticed the red and white roses growing from the hedges she knew what lay before her. Ada didn't want to move forward, but she found herself unable to stop her feet from walking. Her legs continued to carry her to the end of the path then quickly turned to the right.
    She immediately looked up and stared at the statue that loomed over her. The familiar stonework of the likeness of a little girl with her eyes closed towered over her. Ada had seen it too many times before. She had memorized almost every detail of the statue, from the placement of the hands and feet, to the small crack that was present just below the neckline. Ada's left eye caught a bit of movement from behind the large, stone pedestal the statue sat on. She looked to see a small girl slowly walk out from behind it. The girl wore the same blue dress Ada had seen her wear before. The girl brought her index finger up to her lips and gave a small shush to Ada. Then a scream filled the air and Ada looked back up to the statue's face. She could only watch as the statue's eyelids opened to show a pair of human eyes looking at her.
    Ada screamed in terror as she sprang forward out of the bed. "Jesus Christ babe!" Marcus yelled in a half-awake voice. Ada let out several large gasps as her eyes darted around the completely black room. She winced as light suddenly flooded the room. She blinked a few times and let her pupils adjust to it. After a few seconds her vision came back to her and she saw Marcus sitting on the edge of the hotel bed. He held out his arms and gestured for her to come sit next to him. She slowly walked over and sat down next to him.
    He wrapped his arms around her and Ada immediately felt a

sense of safety wash over her. "You had that nightmare again, didn't you?" Marcus asked. Ada simply nodded and Marcus shook his head. "This is crazy babe. This is the fourth night in a row you've woke up screaming your lungs out. What's going on?"

Ada buried her head into his chest and mumbled, "I don't know."

Marcus sighed, "Is something wrong? Cause I'm really starting to worry here."

Ada brought her head up, "No honey, it's just a nightmare. I think it might be because we're traveling."

Marcus rubbed her back, "Well, you've never had nightmares like this when we've traveled before."

Ada shrugged, "It must just be the weather. Everything's so damp and foggy. It's the perfect setting for a horror movie."

Marcus chuckled slightly and let go of Ada while scooting back up to his sleeping spot in the bed. "You may be right about that, but it doesn't get you out of tomorrow's activities."

Ada smiled and moved up next to him. She gave him a quick peck on the lips, "I'm looking forward to them."

Marcus smiled, "Good, now get some sleep," he said turning off the light.

Though she didn't have the nightmare again, Ada was plagued by the feeling of being watched the whole night. She barely got any real sleep, so by the time her and Marcus were headed out she was already tired. As Marcus drove their rental to each new destination she stared out the window. She wasn't focused on anything in particular, and was just staring off in a daze. Her mind was drifting back to that nightmare when Marcus poked her in the side. She jumped a little and woke up from her daze. "Why'd you do that?" she said harshly. Marcus gave her a concerned look before turning his attention back to the road. "Cause you didn't respond to what I asked you," he said in a soft voice.

Ada felt bad for snapping at him, "Oh, I'm sorry. What were you saying?"

An excited smile spread across Marcus' face. Ada could tell that Marcus was pretty excited about their next stop. "I asked if you were ready for the next stop. It's a good one."

She smiled, "Oh really? Well what is it?"

Marcus took in a deep breath then energetically announced, "Our next stop is to the house of Daniel Ravenhurst. He was an upper-class gentlemen of the late nineteen hundreds who made a name for himself in medicine. His medical practice brought him enough money that he was able to build himself a rather large house on an expansive estate."

Ada interjected, "So what's so cool about him?"

Marcus gave her a pouty look and said, "I was getting to that."

Ada held up her hands, "I'm sorry, please continue."

Marcus took a second to remember where he was then continued, "So the guy never had any kids. He never married. Yet, he lived on these gigantic grounds in a house with far more space than he needed."

Ada nodded, "And?" she said trying to get Marcus to the point faster.

"And," Marcus continued, "after a while people started to suspect the good doctor was up to something sinister. People started putting forth weird theories, but the one that stuck was that he was kidnaping his patients and murdering them."

Marcus stopped talking and looked at Ada. She sighed, knowing that he wasn't going to continue until she prompted him to. She rolled her eyes, "So, was he doing it?" Marcus shot her a quick, mischievous look, "That's the funny part. Ravenhurst's patients actually did start disappearing. In fact, seven people who were all his patients vanished. All of them being little girls. They were never able to find the girls, or any evidence to prove it was him. The only evidence that linked Ravenhurst to the disappearing girls, besides them being his patients, was a small, blue ribbon found on his property. His groundskeeper found it and handed it over to police."

Ada asked, "So why didn't they get him?" Marcus shrugged, "I don't think you can arrest someone just for having a ribbon honey. Plus, they didn't have DNA or anything like that back then. There was no way to actually get him for it." Ada turned her gaze to back out the window as Marcus gave a small sigh. "Anyways," he said, "Everyone was so spooked at the notion that he killed a bunch of little girls that no one bought his house after he died. Eventually, it was sold to a historic society who restored everything. It's supposed to be a nice little self-guided ghost tour type deal. Sound pretty cool, right?" Ada halfheartedly nodded, "Yeah, sounds fun."

As soon as they pulled in front of the large estate an unexplainable chill ran through Ada's spine. She felt a sense of anxiety fill her as she stepped out of the car and looked at the large mansion before her. There was something familiar about the place. She couldn't put her finger on it but she felt as though she had seen it before. She was staring so intently at the house that she barely heard Marcus ask, "So where do you want to start?" A small voice seemed to whisper into her ear, "Gardens." Ada said in a dazed voice, "The gardens." Marcus enthusiastically replied, "Sounds good to me! Let's get going."

He took her hand and the two walked forward toward the house. "The gardens are around back," Marcus said as he led them around the side of the mansion. Ada let out an audible sound of amazement as she looked at the large landscape spread out before them. The well manufactured hedges and bushes were spectacular. She was immediately entranced by the incredible array of colors created by all the plant life. She was so taken with it all that Marcus had to lead her by the hand to get them going.

"Alright," Marcus said to himself, "Let's go through this little path here." Ada followed Marcus as he walked toward a set of two long hedges that made up a walking path. As they neared it a familiar sight caught Ada's eye and her heart drop into her stomach. There were steppingstones. Multicolored steppingstones that looked just like the ones from her recurring nightmare. A sense of fear began to wash over her as she stood frozen in place staring at the steppingstones. "Come on honey," Marcus said, "Are you just gonna stand there?" In all honesty, that's what Ada wanted to do, but Marcus wasn't having it. He pulled her by the hand and gently coerced her onto the path.

As they walked down the path Ada saw more and more that she recognized. She felt a lump form in her throat the second she noticed the red and white roses that dotted the hedges they were walking in between. She knew what was up ahead on the right. It wasn't logical for it to be there, but she could feel that it was. She had to know if it was there. She had to face the nightmare. Quickly, she ripped her hand away from Marcus and ran forward down the path. Marcus called something out to her but she ignored it. As she reached the end of the path she bolted to the right and immediately stopped.

There it was standing before her. The same shut stone eyes, the same pedestal, even the same crack just below the neckline. The statue from her nightmare now towered over her in the real world.

She let out a scream of fear and tried to back away but tripped and fell backward to the ground. Ada continued to look up at the statue while letting out wails of terror as she scooted backward on the ground. She bumped into something and cried out in surprise. Tears began to fill her eyes as Marcus touched her shoulders. "What's wrong babe?" Marcus asked. Ada pointed at the statue, "That's it. That's the one from my dreams."

Marcus looked up at the statue and in a confused tone said, "The one from your dream. That can't be. Maybe it looks similar to the one from your dream."

Ada yelled, "It's not! I know it anywhere and it's the one from my dream. It has a crack just below the neck."

Marcus calmly stepped around her and moved forward to study the large garden statue. After a few seconds he said in a leveled tone, "Well...it's there alright. It looks pretty old, so a crack isn't anything crazy." Ada picked herself up off the ground as a small bit of anger mixed in with her fear. Marcus didn't believe her. He wasn't even really listening to her.

Suddenly, Ada heard the small voice from earlier whisper, "Break it." She looked around for the source of the whisper but only saw Marcus. The voice whispered it again, but she tried to ignore it. As she timidly walked toward Marcus and the statue, the voice continued whispering with more urgency. Then, there was another voice chanting the same thing. More and more voices joined in and Ada covered her ears to try to block them out. The voices still made it through to her. Marcus turned to see Ada covering her ears and shaking her head around. "Are you okay?" he asked with genuine concern.

Ada couldn't take the whispers and let out a scream that took Marcus by surprise. She spotted a shovel that the groundskeeper must have left out by accident and picked it up. She ran toward the statue as Marcus stood still in shock. He dove out of the way as she ran by him and swung the shovel and hit the podium. "What the hell are you doing!" Marcus yelled in confusion. The voices whispered to Ada, "The crack. Aim for the crack." Ada let out a shriek and swung the shovel as hard as she could toward the crack in the statue. A metallic ring sounded out and a small chunk of cement fell away from the spot Ada had hit. Marcus stood by in stunned bewilderment as Ada beat the statue with the shovel.

After ten or so swings a large chunk of cement crumbled off

the statue. The voices still told Ada to keep hitting, so that's what she did. Once a few minutes passed, the manic energy that had consumed Ada started to fade away. She was hitting spots of the statue at random and with less intensity. After one final hit she collapsed to her knees and felt the sweat trickle down her face. Ada noticed that the voices had stopped just as Marcus was cautiously approaching her. "Babe? Are you done?" he asked hesitantly. Ada simply nodded and sat there. Marcus carefully bent down and took the shovel gently from Ada, then quickly chucked it away.

Marcus kneeled down beside Ada and put his hands on her shoulders. "Are you okay?" he asked. Ada nodded, "Yeah, yeah I'm okay." Marcus stood up and studied the statue to see how bad the damage was. There were large chunks broken off and cracks all over it now. "Geez babe, you really did a number on this." Something caught Marcus' eye and he leaned in closer to get a better look at it. Something with a semi white color to it was now exposed in the spot that once had the crack Ada had pointed out. It took a few moments for Marcus to realize that he was looking at a bone.

He frantically scanned the rest of the statue and found other pieces of skeleton now showing from the areas Ada had it. He looked at Ada with utter shock, "Th-there's someone in there. There's a body in the statue. I gotta call the police!" Marcus took out his phone and quickly walked a few feet away to call leaving Ada alone in front of the statue. She saw something move from behind the pedestal, the girl from her dream emerged from behind it. For some reason Ada knew her name, "Marisa. It's you, Marisa. You're free from the statue now."

The girl smiled at her and whispered, "Thank you." Then she was gone.

LITTLE GARDEN GNOMES

by Aaron Grierson

A black sedan rolls up to the little villa. Marisa steps out of the car and looks at her Grandparents' house. After pulling her belongings from the back seat she swings the door shut with her hip. The car quickly drives off. Nervous, and new to Spain, she takes a deep breath, slowly walking up the stone path toward her new home.

The lilies and geraniums lining the path in a neat row. Ten or so feet from the house she sees a tall tree with a thick trunk. Nailed to the tree, six feet high is the face of an old man, cast in plastic leaves. Marisa stops to look, raising an eyebrow as she studies the face. Shrugging, she turns and moves toward the house.

She sets her bags down and knocks on the hardwood door. She takes in the sweet, dry smell of the yard and examines the door. The wood is naturally dark, but has paled under decades of sunshine. Within a minute, an old man opens the door.

Stooped somewhere under six feet, he smiles wide, nearly all teeth in place. His skin is deeply tanned and wrinkled, close cropped white hair glinting in the evening sun.

"Marisa! Dulzura! Come in! Come in!" He exclaims, pulling her into a small, energetic dance.

"Abuelo! It's been so long," Marisa says, kissing his forehead. The word leaves her lips like last frost on a new bloom. Spanish feels rusty, but natural to her. Grandpa chuckles.

"My, about fifteen years, if memory serves," he speaks with zest and smiles wider, patting her head like a child. "Come, let's get you settled into your room," he says, grabbing one of the bags and leading her upstairs.

Marisa settles into the guest bedroom, feeling glad she has

reading and Netflix to keep her company. Descending the stairs slowly, with a paper bag in hand, she absorbs the scent of citrus, admiring the antique woodwork and cheery paint job. A smile cracks her lips, excited for life away from the dull greys of her Essex flat. She pulls two figurines from the paper bag, slowly unwrapping them in the kitchen.

"What have you there, sweetie?" Her grandmother glides into the room on soft slippers.

Marisa spins around, clutching a garden gnome tightly in her arms as to not drop it. "Oh Abuela! You snuck up on me!" she sighs deeply, stooping to embrace her grandmother tightly.

"Well the hardwood floors make it easy to glide around," Grandma replies, releasing the hug. "Come darling, let me have a look at you," she says, squinting through thin spectacles. "Radiant! Like sunshine cresting the horizon at daybreak!" she pulls Marisa in, kissing her cheeks. "It's wonderful you got a job so close by. It will be nice to have youth in the house again!" Marisa flushes with embarrassment.

"And I see you've brought some friends for Green Juan in the yard," Grandma leans in to study the garden gnomes.

"Who is Juan? I thought it was just you two," Marisa asks, puzzled. Grandma giggles.

"Green Juan is the tree man," she replies, picking up the other gnome. Marisa's brow furrows further. "You saw the face on the big oak out front, yes?"

Marisa's mouths 'oh', in understanding. Her grandma smiles wide, showing off her dentures. "We'll let them sleep inside tonight and put them out tomorrow. Did you name them?" Grandma says, moving to the fridge.

Marisa pauses for a moment, and pulls out her phone. "Mum said the boy is Oren, 'cause he's so pale, and the girl is Suelita, because her hat looks like a lily." Marisa sits on a stool at the table, studying the gnomes.

"Ah, gifts from your mother? Well I hope they didn't bring that terrible English weather with them!" Grandma says, chuckling again. "For now, let's get you some supper! You must be hungry after the flight." Marisa nods in agreement.

She hears a growl that definitely isn't her stomach. "Uh, Gran? Do you have a dog or a large cat or something?" she asks nervously looking around.

"Oh don't be silly; we're too old for pets. That's just grandpa Hector. Bless him, he only sounds like that when he naps. I worry for you, a young lady in a quiet town," Grandma replies.

Marisa sighs, slumping.

"Oh don't worry about me. I'll get used to the quiet, and the area. I love to walk, I'm happy with books, and have lots of data on my phone. It's good you don't have pets; I'm not sure I could live with a dog after last summer," she begins. Grandma gives her a questioning look. "Oh my roommate had a friend with this Doberman. It wasn't well trained. I had a few... scares."

Grandma nods quietly, "Ah still studious, despite those long legs. Well we have lots of books here if you like. Romance, local folklore, even some history books."

Marisa nods as she grabs Oren, lifting him gently. The pale face is partly hidden by a washed brown beard. It sports a blue outfit that would be baggy if it weren't ceramic, and a bright green hat that flops down behind the head. Suelita has a yellow dress draped over her plump form and a lilac hat which stands nearly straight up. Unsurprisingly, it has no beard, but its gaze seems oddly fixed. Marisa stares intently back, unhappy to lose a child's game to a garden statue.

"All right dear, I've heated some pasta and perch. I hope you like leftovers," Grandma says, setting a bowl down. For a few more seconds, Marisa stares.

She gasps quietly, thinking Suelita blinks.

Convinced she's just tired, she sets the gnome down, moving them both to the other side of the table, facing toward the fridge. She picks up the warm bowl, enjoying the smell. The fish is drowned out with homey spices. Reheated food takes her back to university.

A half moon graces the clear, dark sky, glinting between curtains which sway in a gentle breeze. Marisa shuts her eyes between a vague sense of awareness as she lays quietly in the twin bed. A nightlight glows in the hallway. She draws measured breaths listening to the house. The random creaks unsettle her. Used to the bustle of an English city, the near silence is off-putting.

Sixty six, sixty seven, sixty eight... she counts slowly in her mind. Mum had taught her from a young age to count when trying to fall asleep. Only, instead of counting sheep like normal children, Marisa always imagined little fairies gliding by, inspired by the folklore bedtime stories. A smile creeps across her relaxed lips, amused that the same fairies she grew up with follow her twenty years later, and even across the Channel. They even got her through the break up, although several nights were spent sitting in front of Netflix with ice cream.

Wick-thunk
Wick-thunk

Rolling over, Marisa ignores the noise. It must just be the neighbour's gate.

Wick-thunk
Wick-thunk

Reluctantly, Marisa opens her eyes a crack. The curtain isn't moving any more.

Wick-thunk

It's probably just Grandpa awake from his nap. There was a cane in the kitchen, she thinks.

Wick-thunk

She turns over to watch the hallway, despite shaking her head at her worries.

Wick-thunk

Sighing, Marisa's eyes open a little wider. Surely Grandpa is up the stairs by now? She waits, breathing extra slowly. No more thunking. Only a dull sliding. Maybe he only needs the cane for the stairs? She watches, eyes half open, waiting for him to pass by. Her grandparents' room lies past hers, at the end of the hallway.

Marisa yawns, eyes closing as her mouth stretches. As she reopens her eyes, she sees a small, rounded shadow against the floor. His foot maybe? She squints, hoping to shut her eyes faster when he passes. Her parents always nagged her about not sleeping enough. Her grandparents are probably even worse.

Seconds pass, but the shadow does not. She starts measuring the time with her breathing again, worried something is off. Two seconds in, two seconds out.

In.

Out.

After almost sixty breaths the shadow slowly recedes. She hears the same muffled sliding across the floor and continues to count.

She waits to hear the thunks back down the stairs, but they never come.

A couple of days pass in quiet acclimation for Marisa. She sits on the porch with her nose in a book, enjoying the midday sun. As her grandparents promised, the gnomes sit at the base of the large tree out front. Oren stands on the left, Suelita on the right. Grandma sits a couple of feet away crocheting while Grandpa weeds the flowers.

"Hector!" A man calls from the street. "Keeping those flowers safe from weeds?" All three look up and see their neighbour, Rico and his family standing on the sidewalk.

"Si, si," Grandpa smiles and nods. Rico's son skips up the path between the flowers, keeping an ice cream perfectly balanced in its cone. His wife Amaia dances, moving to the earbuds in her ear. She turns to make cute faces at the baby in the carriage.

Grandpa waves as the young boy approaches. Jorge offers his ice cream, which Grandpa politely declines with another wave. "I just don't want you to get too hot in the sun, senor," the boy squeaks shyly.

"That's all right. This is nothing compared to the heat wave of '55," Grandpa replies with a grin, resting his hands on his knees.

"Fify five?" Jorge asks incredulously. As Grandpa starts talking about the old days, another man jogs by with a lab in tow.

"Gonzalo! Haven't seen you out in a couple of days, man!" Rico greets the newcomer with a firm handshake.

"Yeah the lady has been sick with the flu or somthin' for a week so I've been staying in. Helping her and you know, isolating in case I'm a carrier. Wouldn't want little Jorge or Mia getting sick." He leans in and waves at the baby with a big wide smile.

From the porch Marisa can hear the baby cooing at all the attention. She watches all commotion, earmarking her page. She watches the dog's every move. It is standing alert, focus toward the tree.

Jorge runs back to his parents, afraid of the sudden barking.

Gonzalo looks down at his dog. "Come on, Chico," he says, pulling the leash. Chico continues to bark, pulling against the leash now. "Maybe she sees a squirrel or something. I'll catch you guys later!" He continues down the street, eventually pulling the dog with him.

Rico gives the old couple a look. "Well, we should probably get the kids inside. Don't work too hard, padre!" The family walks toward their home, a few doors down. The old couple wave them off.

Standing as they leave, Marisa walks the yard looking for anything that might have upset the dog. She sees no trace or birds or rabbits in the short grass. Eventually, her eyes fix on the man in the tree. "Green Juan?" she says without thinking. She thinks for a few seconds, back to Mum's tales about the Fae, before checking the gnomes below. The tree remains silent.

Grandma walks up behind her, resting a hand on her shoulder. "It was probably just a bunny or something. Unless perhaps some changlings followed you from home? Juan here is meant as a ward," she explains, squinting a smile beneath the golden sun.

"Abuela! Don't joke like that... they might hear you," Marisa replies, bursting into laughter. "No I don't think anything would want to follow me from home. It's too dry here." She studies her grandma, intrigued by the reference to folklore.

"Oh you're probably right. Those are just fairy tales, darling. I'm not sure anything like that would survive in a world like this. Full of computers, and satellites. Besides, Spain has its own stories, you know like the duendes. They're much uglier than your gnome friends," Grandma's grin grows almost mischievous.

"Haha, you'll have to tell me sometime. I bet I'll need some good stories after working in the field all day," Marisa says.

"Oh, as an archaeologist I bet you'll hear plenty," Grandma replies.

Marisa leans in and hugs her Grandma tightly. "Most of my friends think it's pretty lame."

Grandma scoffs. "Pfft, hard work is anything but lame. The past is important. We can learn so much... But enough of that. Let's talk of Gonzalo, hm? He's about your age."

Marisa rolls her eyes as Grandma pulls her back to the porch.

Rain falls as twilight settles in. Stretching to stand, Marisa finishes yoga in the living room. Her grandparents have just gone to bed. Grabbing her phone, she checks social media one last time for tonight. As she raises the phone, a shadow moves across the living room window. Suspicious, she tucks her phone away, stepping to the window. She checks every side but sees nothing. Maybe it was just a bird overhead. Shrugging, unwilling to go outside in the increasingly heavy rain, she heads upstairs and readies herself for bed.

While brushing her teeth, she flinches as something bangs the window. She stares at it, though the frosted glass and darkness make it impossible to see anything. Marisa spits her toothpaste out in a sigh. It was probably just a tree branch.

As Marisa settles into bed, she quickly falls asleep; calmed by the familiarity of rain, she quickly drifts into a dream.

Marisa's carpool drops her off just after rush hour. She waves at van as it drives away. Slinging a backpack over her left shoulder she walks toward the house. Everything in the yard is pristine despite last night's heavy rainfall. She makes sure the gnomes are at the base of the tree and steps inside. Suelita stands on the left, Oren on the right.

Her grandfather is sitting on the couch watching the 6 p.m. news. "Hi Abeulo!" Marisa says with a smile. He raises a hand to wave but says nothing. She shrugs, setting her bag down and entering the kitchen.

"Abuela! Any excitement around the house today?" she asks Grandma, who is silently staring out the kitchen window at the neighbour watering his plants. "Abuela?"

"No dear, just a quiet day at home. How was work?" Grandma turns to face Marisa, more stiffly than usual.

Marisa smiles. "Oh work was all right. I met the team, there are couple of other new people. We went over the admin and safety stuff, and they showed us around the site but we didn't get to dig. They said the ground was too wet after the rain last night."

"That's too bad. Maybe they'll let you dig tomorrow. That must seem silly, not digging after a little rain. The English dig in the rain," Grandma replies flatly. She chuckles, almost like an afterthought. Marisa laughs too, shaking her head.

"Well we don't want to ruin any potential finds, but yeah the

English are more used to rain, I guess... I'm okay with not working. I don't really love cleaning mud out of my hair and fingernails," she smiles at her Grandma, who stares forward. Not at Marisa but by her. Learning in for a hug, Marisa waits several seconds before Grandma's arms awkwardly fold over her. A woody smell assails her nose as they embrace.

"Are you okay? You look pretty pale despite being outside yesterday. Paler than when I arrived," Marisa says with concern. Another pause. Grandma's eyes shift, blankly staring into Marisa's hazel orbs.

"Of course not, dear. It must just be the lights," she looks up to the ceiling fan which spins weakly around its fluorescent bulb. Before Marisa can reply, she freezes as she hears a *wick-thump* come from behind her.

"I think you bring better news than the TV," Grandpa says, putting a hand on her shoulder. "Haha, Abeulo, that's just because of all the nasty politics around the world right now. You're lucky this town is so peaceful. I saw many protests near the University," she replies, grabbing his wrist. It's stuck firm so she turns and looks. Marisa sees a small, fresh cut. A line of wet silver where blood should be. She lets go, freezing.

"We ordered pizza for seven o'clock so hopefully you're hungry. Be sure to wash up first," he says without enthusiasm.

"Yes, our friends' son recently opened up a restaurant in town. We figured it was time to try it," Grandma says, smiling for the first time tonight.

Are her dentures missing?

Marisa blinks, nodding and spinning as Grandpa's hand finally moves. "Oh that sounds nice! I'll go get unpacked and cleaned up then," she says, hustling upstairs. She washes her face and unpacks her bag before checking the media feeds on her phone. She looks up silver blood in between looking at cute photos.

As 7 p.m. rolls around she watches from an upstairs window as a small car pulls up. Someone steps out, carrying pizza boxes, and she hears the knock on the door. A moment later, the figure is returning, arms freely swaying. She's about to turn away when she notices something small slide across the lawn. A bunny, maybe?

"Dulzura! Come eat while it's hot!" Grandpa calls up. His tone makes the pet name sound nearly dead. Maybe they're totally normal and she's just tired from meeting new people and getting back to work. Shaking her head, she stows her phone. She hops down the stairs, hoping the pizza fixes whatever mood has come over her.

Waking in the middle of the night, Marisa feels still full. The pizza was delicious, covered with fresh meat and veggies and spiced just enough that your mouth burns. She rubs her eyes before wandering to the bathroom.

Coming back in a couple of minutes she stops at the mirror next to her bed. She tries to fix her matted hair. After a few seconds working some knots out, she looks back at the mirror and sees a large shadow looming behind her.

She spins on her heel, nearly falling into the closet.

No one is there.

Quick and quiet she steps out into the hallway.

Empty.

Retreating and sitting on the edge of her bed, she continues to work away at a couple of knots, using them as focus points for breathing. She counts.

Slowly as she can.

It's several minutes before her heartbeat settles down and she crawls back into bed, continuing to count. Only when she lies down do the fairies come and guide her to sleep.

Marisa is up and out of the house before her grandparents awaken. She sits on the lawn, munching on an egg sandwich. Oren is on the left, Suelita is on the right, but several inches away, looking at the driveway.

"Did you two have a fight overnight, or something?" she asks. Falling back into the dewy grass, she laughs at herself for talking to the statues. Instead, she counts Juan's leaves while she waits for the carpool. While counting her thoughts sink back to home, to her so called friends. She had done some stupid things in order to fit in. Why party when she'd rather read a book? Or do drunk karaoke despite not having a singing voice, or a tolerance for alcohol. Or to her ex, who dumped her the same day her application from Cambridge was declined.

The dirty white van finally pulls up. Marisa wipes the tears from her cheek and joins her carpool.

Marisa arrives home within a minute of yesterday, glad to have gotten some sun from working in the field. She steps out of the van and Rico, Amaia and their son Jorge are out walking. "'Ey Mari, welcome home. Working hard out there?" Rico asks, meeting her gaze.

"Yeah, I've missed this work," Marisa responds, sounding tired. She notices the family looks different. Amaia is wearing a loose brown dress, drab for her normal tastes. She walks up to Marisa and hugs her silently. While embraced, she notices Amaia smells her, like a dog. She smells like wood. Ash or maybe cedar. Stepping back, but smiling, Marisa looks over at Jorge. The usually friendly boy is more reserved, carrying some sort of block in his hands. She waves at him, though he ignores her. She looks to Rico, and back to Jorge. Does the boy have the shadow of a beard already?

"Where's your little one today?" Marisa asks Rico, adjusting her backpack.

Rico shrugs. "Oh she woke up feeling sick today, but we wanted to keep to the routine," he explains, his voice flat. Marisa considers this, still smiling. Isn't it odd to leave a young baby unattended for more than a moment?

"I'm sorry to hear. Hopefully it passes quickly," Marisa says genuinely. Their gazes meet again. Rico's eyes seem different. Contacts maybe? Or the setting sun? They just look... dull. Rico and Amaia smile at the same time. The smiles look identical. Like they have matching teeth.

"Well, it was nice to see you. I better get in and washed up before dinner," Marisa says, bounding backwards to the house. "Of course. See you soon. Sleep tight," Rico says, waving his hand stiffly.

The family watches her enter the house, before looking at the gnomes and slowly walking off.

Late at night, torrential rains smack the house, and thunder booms overhead as a storm rolls in. One particularly loud thunderclap wakes Marisa with a start. She lies in bed, panting with that feeling of falling to death in a dream. Listening to the storm, she breathes slowly for a couple of minutes. The odd lightning strike flashes through her curtains.

Unable to fall back to sleep, Marisa wanders into the bathroom. She sips some water and rinses her face. Standing in front of the mirror, she looks at the bags under her eyes. They look the same as they did during exam time. She shakes her head, but applies some moisturizer.

Lightning flashes and in the mirror she sees a gnome dangling from the shower curtain behind her.

Spinning in a panic, she turns to grab the gnome -- but it's gone.

She takes two breaths before retreating quickly to her bedroom. Shutting the door quietly behind her, she pushes the lock in and sets her bag and some dirty clothes in front of it. Hopping into bed she cocoons into the sheets, in spite of the sticky warm night.

Marisa stares at the window, trusting she'll hear the door open. Lightning continues to flash, and she continues to watch, shaking too much to sleep.

As she counts to two hundred, another flash of lightning brightens her curtains, revealing a small shape behind them.

Marisa leaps out of bed, throwing the curtains aside.

Nothing is there.

For good measure, she makes sure the window is shut and locked before crawling back into bed.

Days pass with frequent rainfall. So much water accumulates that work calls the site closed and the trainees can enjoy a break. To keep busy and not spend all day cooped in the house, Marisa walks or jogs through the neighbourhood.

After a few jaunts, she stops leaving the house. Not because of the rain, since she's used to English weather, but the people. Everyone around her has become like her grandparents, or Rico's family. Withdrawn, awkward and staring creepily off into the distance. Or right at her. Like they can see into her soul. Like those damn gnomes!

They're giving her nightmares and maybe even turning her grandparents against her. She feels alone, only safe in her room or at work. She even eats by herself frequently. Her grandparents don't seem to question this, but she feels like she's being watched all the time.

At first, she thought it might have been the rain. Several days in a row felt weird for Spain. But even on sunny days, everyone is the same. It's only been a couple of weeks, but she wishes she could just move back home and forget all this. Last she looked in a mirror, Marisa notices even more white hairs than last month.

"Don't spend too much time out in the rain, you might catch a cold," Grandma says, breaking her bubble.

"I know Grandma, but I'm more worried about you with all this rain. Must be bad for your bones," Marisa replies, turning the chair to face her grandma. Grandma sits in the other chair on the porch. Every movement is stiff, unnatural.

"Oh don't worry about me, these bones know when the rain will fall, and they work just fine," Grandma says, smiling blandly. "We never did thank you properly for those gnomes. They're lovely little garden statues. Talk of the town lately. Please give your parents our thanks," she says.

Marisa pauses, digesting Grandma's words. She inhales, enjoying the smell of wet nature. "Okay, I will. Next time I write home," she finally responds, shifting in her seat.

"I hope that's soon," Grandma says, pulling out another crocheting project. This one looks like a flag full of gnomes. "Don't want to keep them waiting." Her tone is unconcerned, which send a shiver down Marisa's back.

Is that some sort of warning?

Marisa wanders inside, Grandma says nothing as she passes. She emails her parents, letting them know how much her grandparents like the gnomes, but asks if there's anything weird about them, or if there's any association with anything her grandparents mentioned: changelings, green Juan, or John, or men in general. She remembers to ask how things are back home.

The rest of the day passes uneventfully, and the evening looks quiet and clear. So quiet, she doesn't even see Grandpa. Maybe he's tinkering in the basement. Either way, Marisa spends most of her time in her room reading a digital copy of 'Tales from the Lands of Nuts and Grapes,' because it was the easiest book should could find and actually understand.

She's disappointed that there's nothing on gnomes or other

garden statues becoming possessed, or something. Just those creeps Grandma mentioned earlier. She tosses her phone down, running her hands through her curls and rubbing her scalp. The house is dark and quiet now, the sun having set. The smell of an open fire wafts in through the window, something Marisa revels in for a minute while enjoying the scalp stimulation.

Her stomach interrupts the bliss by loudly rumbling. Shaking with sudden hunger, she wanders downstairs into darkness to find some food. Grandma is nowhere to be seen either. Marisa steps lightly as the house is so still.

Flicking the light on, she opens the fridge. Pulling out a bowl of rice, she rummages around for something to have with it. Between the rumble in her stomach and the hum of the fridge, she doesn't hear the approaching *wick-thunks* clattering from the front door. Pushing the door, it remains ajar as she flops onto a stool opposite the fridge.

Sliding across the hardwood floor they approach quickly. From the corner of her eye, Marisa notices something. She turns to see the gnomes, frozen in the threshold. Shutting the door, she breaks eye contact.

They've moved forward a couple of inches.

Feigning calm, Marisa starts shovelling rice into her mouth, watching them carefully. Dripping distracts her, water falling from the faucet. The drops crash loudly into the sink, her nerves on edge in the quiet house.

She stretches, shaking with effort, to shut the tap and stop the dripping. As Marisa overextends, the stool tips.

Yelping, she bangs her head off the counter and the world goes dark.

Marisa wakes up to a smear of green paint. It takes a minute of struggling with her muscles, but she's able to rub her eyes. Everything moves slowly, as she's exhausted and hungry, but finally her vision clears. She stands, wobbling, looking herself over for injuries.

She feels uninjured and sees nothing of worry. What she does see, as she looks out at the world, is a lush forest, a crystalline sky and the sun overhead. Curiously it's not overbearingly bright.

Focusing her gaze, Marisa notices that the trees don't look familiar. They're tall, thick and have an otherworldly glow. As she turns to take in the scene, she spots one small wooden cottage off to her right, and a second one behind. She sways, catching herself. Her hazel eyes glisten with tears.

She stumbles to the first cabin, holding herself together. The wood is pale, emanating a soft glow like the trees in the distance. "Hello?" She shouts, banging on what looks like a door: a five foot high carve out just barely wide enough for her to walk into. Ornate lines of gold wind through it in a script Marisa ponders. "Please help!" she screams. "I'm lost and alone," her voice cracks.

She stops knocking and there is silence for a moment.

Wind kicks up, and noise like a thunderstorm rumbles out of the building.

Flinching, as atmosphere closes around her like a vice, she quickly backs away. Tears run freely down her cheek now, but she walks to the other cottage. It is smaller, made of a dark wood. She finds a similar entrance, only this is inlaid with silver, in the same script. She can't read it, but remembers old stories about the Fae.

As she steps forward to knock, the door swings open on a squeaky hinge. With a deep breath, she considers her options. The forest, while inviting, might be endless. Maybe someone here can help. Straightening up, she steps inside.

THE BUZZ OF A FLY

by David Allen Voyles

    A gentle breeze wafted through the cemetery, gently lifting the pink bloom-laden boughs of the mimosa tree as Marisa ambled among the graves. She felt more at home here at Lakeside Memorial Gardens than anywhere, especially since her mother had insisted on her staying at her grandmother's for the summer. Heavy death metal music played in the ear buds she wore as she ran her fingers lightly over the tops of the tombstones.
    A statue of a little girl caught Marisa's eye, piquing her curiosity enough to draw her over to read the inscription.

Cynthia Lee Davis

b. Feb. 13, 1918
d. July 18, 1930

"I will lend you, for a little time
A child of mine, He said."

- E. Guest

    No way! This little chick died on my birthday? And just twelve years old when she passed.
    Marisa shook her head and studied the sculpted face intently. A memory of her own twelfth birthday, her parents standing by her hospital bed, flashed unbidden into her mind. Pushing the vision away, Marisa pulled the black leather bag with the five-pointed star embroidered with silver studs from her shoulder and sat down in front of the statue. She gazed back up at the little girl and thought, *I wonder if she really looked like that.*
    Marisa fumbled in her bag until she found the small metal pipe with a skull-shaped bowl and a brown pill bottle. She shook out a

single dried bud, packed it tightly into the bowl of the pipe, lit it, and took a long draw on the pipe. Holding the smoke in her lungs, she opened her sketchbook and thumbed through the pencil images she had drawn of gravestones that she had especially liked on her recent walks through the memorial gardens. She blew out a long, blue stream of smoke and set the pipe beside her on the grass, careful not to spill the still-burning ember from the bowl. She studied the statue again and then set to work sketching the girl's face.

Noting the similarity in the length of the little girl's hair to her own she wondered what color the child's hair had been. *Maybe dark, like mine. But obviously not as straight. Bet she would have liked to have had my pink streaks, though.* The chubby cheeks of the little girl contrasted greatly from Marisa's own sharp, narrow features.

As Marisa focused back on the stone figure to get the petite, button nose drawn just right, she gasped.

That freakin' statue just winked at me!

The sketchbook fell from her lap as she frantically jumped to her feet. She took a few steps backward keeping her eyes on the statue. Her heart raced and she realized she was panting as if she had been jogging. The statue looked blankly back at her, as any inanimate figure would.

Damn! Did Raven give me weed that's laced with something?

Marisa snatched up the warm pipe and her sketchbook and approached the statue cautiously. She had a nice buzz going in spite of the scare, a familiar feeling since she frequently enjoyed a single toke from her pipe on walks like this one, but she had never experienced anything close to a hallucination before.

Cynthia Lee Davis stared out with the same sad expression Marisa had observed from the beginning. It was definitely an actual stone statue, not a person posing as one in order to prank innocent passersby as she had seen on the internet. Likewise, nothing in the carved face indicated that the figure could be manipulated like a puppet.

Maybe a trick of the light?

Instead of being frightened, Marisa found that she was more intrigued with the statue than ever. She sat back down and opened her pad, intent on sketching the little girl. Thirty minutes later, she copied the inscription that was carved into the base of the sculpture below the sketch she had made and prepared to leave.

"Well, Cynthia, it's been real. Maybe I'll see you again tomorrow."

"Come play with me, Marisa."

Marisa knew she was dreaming, but it all seemed so real. And she knew exactly who the little girl was who had just invited her to play. Cynthia Lee Davis was alive and vibrant, her dark, wavy hair flying out behind her as she ran along the very path that Marisa had walked earlier that day. She was dressed in an old-fashioned cotton, summer dress that Marisa knew could not be found online or in any department store.

"Let's play hide and seek," Cynthia said. "I'll hide first, and you come find me. Now cover your eyes and count to one hundred before you start looking."

Marisa closed her eyes and began to count. She heard the sound of feet running away from her on the grass, but before she could get to fifty, she heard a squeal. Marisa opened her eyes and turned around in a circle but didn't see Cynthia anywhere. She darted forward in the direction she thought the girl had gone and noticed an above-ground stone monument that looked as if it could have contained a casket. The girl was not hiding behind it. Marisa felt a bit panicked since the sound she had heard the girl make did not seem like a squeal of excitement. She hurried up the row of tombstones looking right and left, and then she heard a distant splash.

Out on the lake not too far from shore, ripples flowed outward from a spot as if a large stone or a heavy bundle had been thrown in. Marisa ran to the shoreline, but couldn't make out anything in the water. She was tempted to wade in, but the water terrified her since she had never learned to swim.

"Cynthia!" Marisa looked back and scanned the cemetery for any sign of movement. Nothing. She called again. "Cynthia!" Still no response nor any sign of movement.

Marisa left the shoreline and ran through the cemetery frantically looking for the little girl. "Ok, you win, Cynthia! Just come out! The game's over!"

There were numerous trees, shrubs, and monuments to hide behind since the cemetery was indeed a garden, but a crypt perched on the top of a small hill caught Marisa's eye. When she got closer, she saw that the lock on the door was hanging loose and that the door was open a few inches.

She pushed the door further into the gloomy interior and stepped inside. Cool, moist air caused goosebumps to break out on her arms and neck. Along the sides there were niches for coffins, and the sun shone brightly through the stained-glass window set in the back wall. On an altar below the window she saw her black leather bag. There was no mistaking that it was hers since the five-pointed star faced her.

How did that get there? She approached it slowly and flipped back the flap to peer inside. Cynthia's stone face stared out at her, just as it had looked in the cemetery earlier in the day. And winked.

Marisa didn't know if she had actually screamed or if that was only in her dream, but she found herself sitting up in bed in the guest room of her grandmother's house panting again as if she had just run a race. Her heart beat so hard she felt that it would surely wake her grandmother if indeed she had not already been awakened by Marisa's scream.

She leaned back on the headboard and waited for her body to recover from the start. She breathed in through her nose and out through her mouth as her therapist had taught her to do when a panic attack struck, and eventually her heartrate returned to a near-normal pace. She heard no sign of her grandmother stirring and was relieved that she had not actually screamed aloud.

Glad I don't have to explain that to Nana. Mom would be insisting on a drug screen for sure. Marisa turned in the bed to reach for the bedside lamp to read a bit more of the dark fantasy novel in the hopes that she would fall asleep soon.

The sound of footsteps coming down the hallway toward her room made Marisa freeze.

Spoke too soon. Nana's up, after all.

But then Marisa noticed something odd about the footsteps.

That sounds like bare feet. Nana wouldn't be caught dead without her pink slippers.

The soft slap of flesh on the bare wood floor of the hallway was unmistakable. But there was something more to the sound that made Marisa's flesh crawl. Something dripping.

Even though Marisa had not had time to turn the lamp on, the moonlight from the window gave off enough light to see the room fairly well. The door to the hallway slowly swung open. Standing in the doorway was a child. Even in the moonlight Marisa could see that the girl's clothes were sopping wet. Water still streamed from the long, soaked strands of hair and dripped onto the floor.

It was Cynthia. Her pale skin held a soft blue glow from the moonlight, but the most frightening thing of all was that her eyes were as blank as the orbs behind the lids of her graveyard statue.

"Come play with me, Marisa."

The next thing Marisa knew, she was waking up with the sun shining brightly though her window. What had happened in the interim she could not remember.

Marisa felt compelled to return to Lakeside but found herself strangely drawn to visit Cynthia's statue while at the same time wishing to avoid it. She deliberately took the path that wound down to the lakeshore where she noticed a boy probably close to her own age skipping rocks along the surface of the water.

Normally she went the other way when she found herself likely to be forced into social interaction in the park, but there was something about the dark-haired young man that intrigued her. His clothes were odd, a plus in Marisa's book.

Cool. No blue jeans and T-shirt for this guy, she thought. *Probably works the second-hand stores.* She looked down her body at her own outfit consisting of a black t-shirt (this one featuring *Kittie*, an all-girl 90's goth band), black jeans, and her trademark cherry red Doc Martens. She decided she would continue on the path and see if he spoke. At her approach, he nodded at her and smiled.

"Hi."

"Hi," Marisa echoed. "You're pretty good at that." She glanced out at the water where the ripples from his last throw were fading away.

"Lots of practice," he said. "How about you?"

"Nah. I just come here for the quiet. And to sketch a little. There are some pretty cool tombstones here."

"You're an artist?"

Marisa shrugged. "I draw."

"Can I see?" The boy pointed to the sketchbook.

"Sure. But it's not that good. Just stuff I see that interests me. I tell myself I'll work up the ones I like the best, but for now…" her voice trailed off.

"I'm Ian," the boy said, as he walked toward a grassy area away from the shore a bit. He motioned for her to sit and then sat down himself.

"Marisa." She handed him the sketchbook and he immediately opened it and slowly worked his way through the drawings. Marisa stared out over the water to hide her interest in his reaction.

"You lied to me," he said. Marisa's head snapped back toward him. "These are really good." Marisa blushed but smiled.

"Thanks."

"Hey, I know this statue," Ian said pausing at the sketch of Cynthia Lee Davis. "It's not far from here."

Marisa shivered as she remembered her dream from the night before. "Yeah, I, uh, thought it was…interesting."

"What's the quote for?" Ian asked.

"It's on the statue," Marisa said. "I guess her parents wanted it. I looked it up. It's from a poem by a guy named Edgar Guest. A lot of people whose kids have died have it inscribed on their tombstones. Like Cynthia's. Kinda weird, if you ask me."

"What do you mean?"

"Well, I guess some parents are comforted by the idea that their child was so special that God gave it to them for just a little while. Like it was too precious to be here on the Earth for long. But it just seems cruel to me. I mean, what kind of god would give a kid to people only to take it away a few years later. Seems like a mean, petty thing to do. Like what a devil would do. Not God."

Ian nodded thoughtfully. "Yeah, I see your point. So you're not only an artist, but a philosopher, too."

Marisa snorted. "Hardly. I just think about death a lot, I guess." She gestured at her clothes. "Like you couldn't tell that."

Ian laughed. "I think about death a lot, too." He smiled at Marisa in a way she didn't know how to take, so she let the silence hang in the air. "My sister died. Drowned in this lake."

Guilt washed over Marisa in a hot wave. "I'm sorry. I wouldn't have brought it up if I'd known."

"Ah, forget about it. That was a long time ago." He really didn't seem upset which Marisa didn't quite know how to take. "We all are going to die sometime so we might as well not be afraid of it."

"You're not afraid? To die?"

Ian shook his head and smiled again. "What's to fear?"

"All kinds of stuff," Marisa said. "Hell. Demons. A lake of fire."

"Sounds like somebody's been a bit naughty."

That made Marisa laugh. "I think what I really fear that's maybe worse is that there's nothing after you die. That this is all there is." They both sat in silence for a moment, watching a group of ducks paddle near the rocky shore looking for small fish.

Ian turned his attention back to the sketchbook and flipped through a few more drawings. He stopped at a drawing of a fly.

"This one's a bit different. Not about death at all."

Marisa saw what he was looking at and frowned but felt comfortable sharing why it was important to her since Ian had revealed such a personal fact with her.

"I had a dream once," she explained, "that I had died and my parents were there in the room with me, like a wake. I was dead but aware of everything going on. They were talking like nothing had happened. Other people would come and go, stay for a bit to visit, eating and chatting and laughing. Only it was weird. I could see them talking, but I couldn't hear them. It was totally silent in the room. Seeing everybody talking and laughing was just so strange and sad; it was like they didn't care at all that I had died. Nobody cared. Even the preacher just laughed and ate food. It was like even God didn't care. And through it all, like I said, it was quiet. Except for one thing."

Marisa took a deep breath, and Ian tilted his head to study her. His look was intense, but compassionate.

"There was a fly in the room, and I could hear its buzzing. That was the only thing I could hear. Like that was the only thing that cared." She gave a sad, little chuckle. "Or maybe it didn't care at all either. Not even a fucking fly."

Ian blew out his breath. "That was some dream!"

Marisa looked at Ian and feeling a moment of closeness that she couldn't explain, blurted out the question she had been wanting to ask.

"So, do you think there's a heaven? Or God?"

"God?" He studied her silently for a moment. "No, I don't think so. At least, I hope not." He paused again to let that sink in and then offered a smile so chilling it made Marisa shiver. "On the other hand, an afterlife? Oh, yes. Most definitely. But not necessarily heaven."

Marisa heard the footsteps again that night. She pulled the covers over her head as she had done when she was little, and listened, trembling, in the darkness. She heard the squeak of her bedroom door opening, and the smell of decay and of wet clothes that had been left to sour in a moldy pile filled the room. Then the soft, wet padding of bare feet walking around the foot of the bed that stopped only when they reached her side.

"Go away," Marisa whimpered from under the covers.

Silence.

She heard only the sound of her own short, shuddering breaths. She forced herself to breathe slowly in through her nose and out through her mouth. When she felt calmer, she slid the covers down past her chin and opened her eyes.

Inches from her own face, the dripping, wet face of the twelve-year-old girl, her eyes as blank as a stone statue, grinned at her.

"Come play with me, Marisa," she whispered.

Marisa shut her eyes and whimpered into the covers she clutched at her mouth. When she dared to open her eyes again, the girl was gone.

The next day Marisa was back at Lakeside. She walked her familiar route among the graves, hoping that she would spot Ian. Their parting had seemed odd given his strange, unsettling remarks about God and the afterlife, but she found him extremely compelling and provocative. And if she were totally honest, attractive in several ways.

Her path took her past the statue of Cynthia Lee Davis. Marisa's stomach churned but forced herself to look into the statue's face as she kept her steady but slow pace. She fully expected the stone features to change, to wink or maybe even sneer. But the face remained frozen in its emotionless gaze. When it became awkward to look back at the statue, Marisa turned toward the lake, hoping she would see her new friend.

When she got to the shoreline she looked in vain both ways; there were no other people in sight. Letting out a big sigh, Marisa plopped down on the grassy bank and stared at the water. She thought about sketching the lake scene that stretched out before her, but her heart just wasn't in it. She tossed her sketchbook to the side and hugged her knees as she peered at the water.

"Hey!"

Marisa hadn't heard Ian approach and jumped a bit at his sudden greeting.

"Sorry. Didn't mean to startle you."

Marisa smiled sheepishly and stood up while brushing the grass and dirt from her rear.

"I was hoping you would be here," she said.

"Really?" Ian said. "That's good because I have something to show you." He reached for her hand and Marisa let him take it. She was surprised at the thrill she felt by that simple contact, the touch of his hand in hers.

After walking a short way along the shore, Ian suddenly stepped into the water.

"Hey, what are you doing?" Marisa yelled, half-laughing and half-annoyed. When Ian kept walking further into the lake, her amusement dissolved completely. "Ian! What the hell are you--!" She tried to jerk her hand free but Ian held firm as he continued to walk out into the lake. The water was quickly up to their waists, and Marisa thrashed at him with her free hand.

"Damn it, Ian, this isn't funny! Let me GO!" No matter how much she struck at him while trying to free herself, he held his grip on her and continued to go further into the lake. In seconds the water was closing over their heads. Ian wrapped both of his arms around Marisa's as he pulled her under the water with him.

From the slight rise of the hill that overlooked the lake, the statue of Cynthia Lee Davis watched as the splashing from the struggle subsided and the ripples emptied onto the shore.

"Hey, folks, just wanted to let you know I'll be locking the gates soon." The couple that had been reading the epitaph on the memorial turned toward the speaker.

"Oh, I thought the park was open 'til sunset," said the russet-bearded man.

"Normally it is, that's right," said the caretaker. "But with recent events the city's decided to close early for a while."

"Recent events?" the blond woman asked.

"Yeah…" the park custodian hesitated as if unsure whether to say more. "A girl in the area disappeared a few days ago. The police aren't sure that it's foul play but they want to play it safe. You've still got some time to look around; it'll probably take me fifteen minutes or so before I make it back up to the gates."

"Ok, thanks," the man said. The caretaker walked back over to the jeep he had left idling and drove slowly off down the paved cemetery road.

"That's kind of creepy, huh?" said the woman.

"Yeah. Almost as creepy as this statue."

"What do you mean? It's just a little girl." The woman squinted as she looked again at the sculpture.

"I don't know, she just seems kinda weird to me. I mean, according to the marker, she was twelve when she died. But this girl's face seems older than that. The clothes look right but that straight hair? Not the style for 1930. And that narrow face with the sharp nose? Just doesn't look right to me."

"Yeah, maybe," the woman responded. "But the inscription is *definitely* creepy." They turned their heads to the base of the statue in unison and read it silently.

"I heard a Fly buzz – when I died –"

- E. Dickenson

The couple turned and made their way to their car. Behind them a single tear coursed down the stone cheek of the statue that no longer resembled Cynthia Lee Davis.

REFUGE

by Elias Baum

It was like waking from a dream. My thoughts slowly reassembled themselves from all around me; a cloudy haze of disjointed memories sharpening into a single focused point of light. Then, I became aware of myself. I inhaled, the sweet smell of summer washing over me. I'd been daydreaming, or distracted, or nodding off. I was sitting at a small wooden desk next to a window. I'd been looking down at a piece of paper and holding a pencil. The sunlight was warm on my skin, growing dimmer for a moment as a cloud passed the sun.

Through the window I saw a vast green field , dotted with houses, stretching out into a dark line of trees a great distance away. There didn't appear to be any roads, or any discernable method as to how the houses were placed. They were scattered about, almost haphazardly. I wasn't sure how long I'd been sitting there, or how I'd come to find myself in that place. I'd recently been somewhere else, someplace I'd felt afraid, and I felt this place was safe. I sat and looked out that window for what seemed a long time, basking in the stillness.

I was inside a small, finished cabin. The walls were thick logs stacked one upon the other, and as the sun danced from cloud to cloud, the atmosphere of that single room shifted from a shadowy calm to a welcoming afternoon glow. The only features were the desk where I sat, two open windows, one each to my left and right, and an open doorway behind me. I could hear the wind outside, rushing through the sky, and the creak of the wooden chair as I turned in my seat.

The breeze lifted the corner of the paper sitting on the desk, which jarred me from my passive observations and forced me to engage, almost unconsciously, as I brought my hand down to keep it from flying away. Pulling my arm back, I saw that the surface of the desk was scarred with age and use. It looked almost exactly like

a desk I'd used in high school. I set the pencil down and examined the paper. It was crinkled and yellowed with age, and had been torn from a notebook. Something had been written on it.
I made this place for you, Marisa. Make it whatever you want.
It was my handwriting, and my name. Had I written this? My eyes flicked to the pencil I'd been holding. The lead was worn though I didn't remember writing with it. I read the paper again.
I made this place for you, Marisa. Make it whatever you want.
A sense of euphoria washed over me. Had I *made* this place? A place where I could sit and write, and think, in solitude, for hours, or days, or years; however long I cared to be here? I breathed deeply and exhaled, feeling a sense of peace I hadn't felt in a long, long, time. I stood up from the desk, a lingering soreness in my legs. I stretched, my arms reaching high into the air, and walked to the doorway. It was a perfect summer day. The green fields ran on and on, and the only sound was the wind. Despite the houses scattered about, I somehow knew that I was utterly, wonderfully, alone.

I surveyed my little kingdom; a place that could be whatever I wanted it to be. My eyes lingered on the houses, looking from one to the next, the closest of which was probably a half-mile away. It felt familiar somehow, though I couldn't immediately understand why. Realization came as I recognized its long, dark, porch, its gray front door, and the small triangle-shaped window near the roof. I *knew* that house.

I had been in the attic of that place, with someone I knew. She had been older than me, maybe eight or nine. I couldn't remember her name, only that she always seemed a little sad when we played. She'd had a small plastic truck. It had been red, or maybe blue. Something she'd said once came to me. She'd said she "liked to hide in the attic sometimes." I hadn't thought about those things for a long, long time, and was surprised by their sudden presence in my mind.

My attention shifted to another house, a little further away, behind the first. The only thing I could really make out was its bright pink color, which was all I needed. I remembered that obnoxious pink place and the old lady that lived downstairs. She'd rented the upstairs to my younger sister and her boyfriend. My mom had been angry she'd started dating and tried to stop her, which just drove her out of the house and into his arms. They'd moved in together, in the upstairs of that pink house. That's where he'd gotten her into drugs, and then left her, pregnant and alone. I'd hated the color ever since, almost blaming it for what happened.

I looked over to my right and saw a leaning, weather-beaten, filthy old trailer. It still had that tall brown fence around the back, a dented metal trash can out front, and a large wiry antenna hanging awkwardly to one side. I hadn't thought about that place in a long time, either. I hadn't wanted to. Walking in and finding my mother slumped over, sitting in the chair that had become a sort of refuge for her, in a place without family. She'd been alone, her TV playing, a daytime talk show droning on over her body. Her small side table was covered in toppled prescription bottles and loose pills. That trailer had been demolished years ago. Yet, here it was, looming over me, from a distance. The breeze blew by me again, colder than before. I walked back into the cabin, and sat down at the desk.

I made this place for you, Marisa. Make it whatever you want.

This certainly wasn't what I wanted. The things outside were things I'd abandoned or forgotten years ago, some unconsciously with the passing of time, others by choice, with the passing of responsibility. I couldn't have saved that little girl from her sadness, I couldn't have saved my sister from her choices, and I couldn't save my mom from her mind. I wasn't responsible for the choices others had made.

The wind rippled the edge of the paper again, and I noticed there was something written on the back. I turned it over.

You ruined this place, Marisa. You brought it with you.

My handwriting again. I'd brought it with me. I quickly flipped the paper back over and saw what had been written before was gone. Now, there was only a single line.

It's still hunting you.

A strong gust rushed against the cabin, violently sweeping through the windows. My eyebrows furrowed, and I took a breath. I picked up the pencil and ran the lead back and forth across that line until I couldn't see it anymore. It was blotted out in a dark torrent of ragged frustration.

I looked out onto the field. Everything there suddenly carried with it a sense of the ominous and alien. The houses became black teeth sheltering hidden things. The fields became the lair of some lurking evil. Even the sky hung heavier with its menacing and cloudy blue, lingering over me, sending the wind right through me. The light was dimmer as the afternoon sun had given way to a shadowy dusk. That single sentence had been the introduction of doubt into my tiny little paradise. I felt a tinge of fear.

I looked back at the paper. Beneath my hurried scribbling the line had been written again.

It's still hunting you.

I scratched the new line out, and flipped the paper back over, hiding those angry dark blots from my view. When I did, I instinctively pushed the paper away and let out a yelp. The words were gone. They'd been replaced, not with another message, but a crude illustration, a child's drawing. It was a face, all teeth and grin and menace, leering at me, exactly as I'd drawn it so many times before.

The paper slipped from the desk and landed with that horrible image face down. On the reverse side, both of my scribbled out markings were now gone, replaced with another single sentence.

It's here.

"We have to go," said a small voice from behind, startling me.

I turned and saw a little girl; my playmate from so many years ago. The little girl from the attic. She stood in the doorway, wearing dirty, brown sweatpants and a long-sleeved gray shirt that was too large. Her sleeves were rolled up, and her hair was a disheveled and dirty mess of stringy blonde. She was holding a plastic truck in her right hand. It was green. She looked like she'd been crying.

"We have to hide," she said, urgency in her voice. Her eyes spoke a tragic sense of necessitated fear no young child should ever come to know.

"Where?" was all I could think to say, but something in my heart had already begun to understand.

Then I heard it.

At first I thought it was something rattling back and forth on some far off porch, maybe a clumsy wind chime, swinging in the breeze, radiating its metallic resonations. It faded, but then there it was again, more noticeable, louder. It became more rhythmic, a machine sound, a repetitive striking, like pistons, churning up and down, up and down, and it was drawing closer.

The girl turned and ran. I didn't say anything, just followed her out the door. We ran out beneath the immense canopy of summer twilight. The sun was now low in the sky, casting long shadows from the houses which seemed to chase us across the fields. The girl was remarkably fast, her little legs pumping as fast as they could carry her. Even though I was much older and larger, I had tremendous difficulty keeping up with her as she fled. It was an animal fear that drove us—the thing hunting us much larger, much stronger, undaunted, and unrelenting. The sound grew louder still, and I knew it would never stop chasing us.

In my haste I hadn't seen where she was running, but then realized we were heading toward the large house with the long, dark porch, the gray front door, and the attic. Something in me screamed to turn away, to stop her from leading us there. I felt if we ran there we would be found, we would be forced to confront the thing chasing us, and it would destroy us. I wanted to warn her, to tell her to stop, but she was running so fast and so hard, and I was out of breath, and I couldn't speak.

Another sound came to me then, carried by the wind. It was a wailing, sobbing, cry, coming from the pink house. It sounded like my sister. She had screamed when she learned she was pregnant, and she had screamed when she had the abortion, but not when she took the pills that ended her life. The screams blended with the breeze and became something else. They weren't the angry cries of my sister, but those of my mother, filled with agony and grief. Her voice reached right out from a place I couldn't see, just like the cold wind that had blown through me, chilling me to the core, burrowing directly into a heart that had chosen *not* to remember, but had never forgotten.

Those screams stirred in me a sleeping agony, prompting me to run with everything I had left, as the little girl quickly climbed the three wooden steps that led onto the long, dark porch, ran down the length of it, and up to the gray front door. She pushed it open and I followed her in, quickly slamming it closed, shutting out all light from the outside. The world became black and white; a grayscale nightmare of the hunter and the hunted. I was in a place that I both knew and didn't know; a hazy, distant, memory, from decades ago when I was only a little girl. I remembered being here, *living* here, and hiding in the attic.

The wind outside had vanished entirely, as had the mournful cries of my mother's grief. All I could hear was the encroaching presence of the hunter, step after step after step, coming for me. The thing whose face I'd seen on the back of that crumpled, yellowed, paper in the cabin. I thought I'd defeated it, put it behind me, but it had continued to follow me, seeking me out, and now it was here, and I was trapped again.

Almost as if she knew what I was thinking, the little girl turned to look at me.

"We have to get up there," she said, and pointed at the ceiling. "It's dirty, but there's a spot in the corner that's mostly clean. That's where I hide." The girl pulled the long, dingy, gray string that brought the attic ladder down. She climbed up and disappeared into the dark. As I started to climb, I risked a quick glance toward the front of the house. Through the window I thought I saw the outline of the thing lurching toward us in the last shadows of dusk. I desperately clambered up after her. Once in the attic, I heaved the dropped ladder up from the ground, sealing us inside with a loud slam.

I coughed at the sudden cloud of dust as the silence consumed everything but our ragged breathing. As my eyes adjusted I looked around, trying to see where she'd hidden. It was difficult to see, the only light now coming in through the triangle-shaped window set near the center of the house. Night had come and the moon had risen, filling the space with a low-lit glow, which reflected off the low-hanging beams of dusty rafters and tufts of insulation.

"Over here," I heard her whisper. "There's room for you, too."

The attic seemed so much larger when I was a child, so vast and cavernous. Now it felt tight, constricting, and I wasn't able to lift my head. I was too large to hide here. I needed to find someplace else.

"There's no time," the girl said, from the dark, answering my thought.

Calming my breathing, and keeping my face low to the floor, I slowly crawled over to where I'd heard her voice. As I drew closer I saw the slight outline of her face in the moonlight. I could only make out one cheek, and some of her hair dangling over a single eye, which was wide and filled with fear. "Come on," she whispered.

I pulled myself in next to her, folding my legs into my chest to fit into our hiding spot. I was surprised I was able to fit into such a tiny space. We were wedged between a beam and a pile of things stacked tightly to my right. The machine sound from earlier was gone, replaced by the vacuous ringing of sudden silence. We watched, listened, and waited. Dust particles floated through the single beam of moonlight coming in through the window, finding its resting place on the closed attic door.

"I don't hear it," I whispered.

She put a finger to my lips, shushing me. I could still only see half of her face. She glared out at the moonlight, the door, and then back at me. The fear was still there, but I could tell she was trying to be confident. I felt braver knowing she was with me.

I listened, trying to hear if the thing had followed us in, had come in the door, or if it was walking around below. I heard nothing. I felt a painful spasm in my right leg, cramping from being in such an awkward position. I tried carefully stretching both legs out but brushed up against the pile of things stacked to my right. I looked back at all the boxes and junk, shadows of things stored away and forgotten, and tried to ease the tension in my legs. Then my eyes fell on something that caused me to inhale sharply, forcing the little girl to cover my mouth with her hand.

I only half-heard what she whispered as I struggled against her, my breathing erratic. I stared at the face leering at me from the darkness, a face that was all teeth and grin and menace. It was the face of the illustration, the face I'd drawn again and again as a child. Here it was, next to me, the very thing. To others it was nothing more than an ugly, gray, crouching, garden statue, a thing of decoration. For me it was the face of the hunter; the all-encompassing embodiment of an experience from my childhood, manifested.

It began hunting me when I was six, on a night when my father had come home, filthy, angry, and drunk beyond measure, looking for someone to hurt. My older sister and I hid in the attic like we had many times before. This time he found us. He'd beaten my sister lifeless, his large arms coming down on her tiny body, repeatedly, relentlessly, like the pistons of an unfeeling, inhuman, emotionless, machine. After he finished with her, he turned to me, landing blow after blow, knocking the memories away, until nothing of my sister, my father, or that night remained. It was all lost in a cacophony of tears, shouts, and my pregnant mother's screams.

I had been counseled and coached into abandoning every memory of that horrible event. Despite other's best efforts, there were still two things I remembered: the face of that statue, which had replaced everything I knew of my father with that cold, stone, tooth-filled grin, and the distant wailing of my mother. The face of the statue had *become* the face of my father, and I'd drawn it for years, a horror imagined, reimagined, remembered, and toyed with, in the scribblings of a wounded child.

"Marisa, we *have* to be quiet. He's *listening* for us."

Then, I was six again. My older sister's hand over my mouth, making it hard for me to breathe as I pushed away from that horrible face in the dark. I felt so small, so tiny, next to my sister, and I didn't truly understand what was going on, only that there was a large and scary face next to me and we had to hide, and I didn't know why, and I didn't want to be next to that *thing*. I kicked at it, my feet hitting rafters and boxes, knocking them to the floor. My erratic breathing continued, heightened, a tiny desperate gasp in all that darkness.

Then I heard pounding on the attic door. My sister jumped, and her hand left my face. I saw the boards of the attic door begin to break. I knew that our father was going to come through that doorway in a moment and destroy me, destroy us, destroy our family, forever. There was nowhere to go, nowhere to run, and nowhere to hide. I reached for my sister's hand.

I looked at her, in those last moments, and thought I saw a solace in her eyes, that we were together. Her eyes turned away just as the door was breached, the wooden boards falling away, revealing a dark space into the house below. I saw the outline of the thing, the hunter, the unfeeling machine-man, the beast, my father, who I had long associated with the face of that statue, a thing discarded and stored in a forgotten loft, forever burned into my memory. It was here, it was now, and it was the dark silhouette climbing up into the attic, moving toward me and my older sister. We screamed, too small to do anything but shout as his brutal and vicious hands reached for us. "Daddy, no!"

Then I woke up.

THE WHITE LADY

by Zachary Finn

Lake Ontario stretched out toward the horizon, a seemingly never ending expanse of rippling blue, greys, and whites forever at odds with each other. As the water swirled and crashed, Marisa sat on the rocky beach peering out over the lake. The sun was just beginning to descend toward the waterline, and the sky transformed into a series of orange and purple stripes hinting that dusk was approaching. A soft fall breeze carried across the water and rippled through Marisa's hair as she watched it all unfold and got lost in her thoughts.

Somewhere down the beach, a young man walked by himself admiring the same sky and breeze as Marisa. His hands were in his jean pockets as he strolled along the deserted beach. *Funny*, he thought to himself, *a few years ago you couldn't* pay *me to walk on this beach without someone.* Like all children who grew up near Durand Eastman Beach, there was an almost reverent fear of being caught alone out there-- let alone as night was approaching. As the colors of the dusk sky grew deeper, Jeff stopped and took in the surrounding scenery.

The beach was still empty, as it had been since he'd arrived. Littered across its sand was a mix of driftwood, shells, rocks, and the occasional rubble of a fire long since burned out. The beach itself was little more than a twenty foot strip, which was surrounded by the Great Lake on one side and a steep incline covered with trees on the other. It was one of the reasons Jeff wanted to come back; there was a sense of isolation, of being completely *alone*, that was hard to find in so many other places. When it was void of people, as it strangely so often was, it seemed as if the space was transported to another time, or maybe, it was outside of time. The ledge of trees provided the perfect blockade from the paved pathway and benches that existed on the other side, while the Lake's meandering coast seemed to extend for an eternity in the distance. The beach *felt* desolate, and for Jeff that was just fine: it made it easier to muse about his childhood love of

Durand Eastman, and the past in general, as the waves lapsed softly near his feet.

Alone with his thoughts he started walking again. To his left, about thirty feet in the distance, was a break in the veil of trees. Like a plug being pulled from a cask, the sandy beach seemed to pour from the break in the foliage, spilling out to the area that lay beyond. He picked up his pace, excited to see if what the sandy path led to was the same as it had been when he was a child. He labored with each stride, his feet sinking deep into the sand, but it would all be worth it if he could see *her* castle. The White Lady's Castle, that is.

Marisa watched as the young man began picking up his pace, she had only noticed him moments before and was curious. There was an almost childish glee to his gait. Sand sprayed behind him with each lunge forward, and he pumped his arms wildly to counter the shifting floor beneath him. He was well dressed, wearing a pair of jeans, a light blue dress shirt, and a grey sweater over the shirt-- all of which seemed out of place on the beach; however, the crisp October air made the layers necessary. His curly brown hair blew wildly about from both the sea breeze and his sudden movements, which only added to the perception of childlike excitement. Marisa let out a deep sigh of interest as she pried her gaze away from the young man toward the fall sky, which continued to grow darker.

Jeff rounded the makeshift corner of trees and there it was, sitting across Lake Shore Boulevard. When he was younger it might as well have been Warwick Castle with how large and intimidating it seemed; now however, it appeared little more than a decaying wall thrust atop a hill in an overgrown forest. He fell momentarily crestfallen as the reality of what the castle was overpowered his childhood memories, but it only lasted for a second. *Of course you remember it differently, you were a kid then. That doesn't make it mean any less. Besides, it was the story that made it something, not the structure,* he told himself. He *needed* to convince himself, after all. How else was he ever going to get past this damn writers block? The whole reason he was there was to jog his memory to some past moment or experience, some feeling, which he could then put to paper to move the plot of his most recent book forward. *You have to get out of this rut,* he reminded himself, *take everything in. Think about how this place made you feel when you were younger and first heard that story.*

He thought back to sitting in his fourth grade class. Mrs. Evan's had read about ancient Egypt in class earlier that day, which had spurred a rousing lunchtime discussion about curses and the like. It was little Mikey Shultz who had told him the story of the White Lady in a way only a fourth grade student could:

"Her daughter got murdered by a gang way back in the old days, and they hid her body so no one could ever find her," Mikey had claimed after they'd pushed their Styrofoam plates still covered with various cafeteria mush aside. To aid in his storytelling, Mikey had even taken a sheet of paper and pencil out from his backpack to illustrate. "And the White Lady spent *allllll* her life looking for her. She lived by the beach, and every night she'd light her lantern and she'd bring her two dogs out with her, calling for her daughter as she wandered. She never found her, and eventually she died of a broken heart in her castle." It was then that Mikey started sketching his interpretation of the White Lady's Castle as he continued with the story. "Now she haunts the whole area, woods, beach, castle n' all. Anyone walking around the area at night who's evil, she takes to her castle and," he pointed to the top of the castle he'd sketched, "shoves them off the top 'till they die!" To illustrate the point, he drew a heap of stick figures with their eyes crossed out at the bottom of the sheet.

"How do *you* know?" Jeff had asked almost immediately after Mike was done telling his story. "My brother went," was the sufficient reply. Mikey's brother was in middle school and knew a lot, so that all about ended any further questioning. Of course, less than a week later Mikey, Jeff, and a group of friends whose names he had long since forgotten, had ridden their bikes to the castle during the day to explore. They'd tromped about the whole area looking for signs of a ghost, but spent the better part of the time at the castle. Back then it seemed a megalithic structure, dominating the landscape with tiers and gunnery towers surely designed to punish evil-doers. The cobbled wall seemed an impenetrable, evil fortress surely befitting the White Lady in her quest for vengeance. Needless to say, they'd scampered back home at the first hint of dusk.

As Jeff thought back to that day, it seemed the realities of what he'd seen had somehow blended with little Mikey's drawing, as he remembered it towering over him in a display of forbidden power. Stranger still, Jeff had visited the area countless times after, even as late as high school going to bonfire parties and drinking on the beach, but it had always been ingrained in his adult memory as it had seemed to him that first trip back in fourth grade. Back when a giant haunted castle *could* exist on the shore of Lake Ontario, and not an old, crumbling wall probably built in the 20th century for a park, or picnic patio, or something mundane like that. From the front the castle, *or wall*, he thought more aptly, was about twenty feet high. It had been built into a steep hill, which placed it an additional twenty feet higher than ground level. In the center there was a giant bulge jutting out, which appeared to be an attempt to create a chemise that would also act as an overlook. Also at each end of the structure were two small cylinder shaped towers that similarly served as vantage points for visitors. It wasn't what he remembered, but clearly whoever built this thing was *trying* to evoke the appearance of a castle, even if it was underwhelming when compared to how he remembered it. *I'm here, might as well go see it up close,* he figured. Jeff took a deep breath, fearing the stroke of inspiration he was hoping for might never occur, and began walking toward the castle.

There was a brief, white-hot moment of rage that filled Marisa's chest as the young man continued his journey toward the wall. Why? Why can't they just leave it alone? But the anger passed almost immediately, and she decided to follow. She followed as he walked past the parking lot, crossed the road, and began walking up the stairs with interest. Marisa had watched each of those things as they'd been built over the years, and though the "castle", as she'd heard it been called, had no connection to her, it did *encompass the old plot of land that had been her mother's all those years ago.*

Her mother.

There was a time when Marisa had watched her mother and the dogs she'd gotten after her... incident... search the beach nightly calling out her name. How many decades or centuries ago that had ended was lost to Marisa as years blurred together, but she knew somehow her mother had turned into a local myth. They visitors were always talking about "the White Lady" whenever they came, and sometimes she would hear them screaming that same name before she'd find the bodies, though Marisa never found out what had killed them. Not that it mattered. She was a watcher, a gazer, who stayed watching the shore as she had when she was alive. Sometimes she'd wander through the woods like she had; or sometimes she'd listen to conversations that were happening with an eavesdropper's interest; there was a freedom and sense of wonder that she freely explored.

And now, she was interested in following the well-dressed young man to the castle.

Jeff turned the corner from the cement staircase built into the hill and surveyed the back of the castle. The wall from this side was barely over three feet high, and consisted of the same cobbled stone as the front. "At least there's a view," Jeff said to himself as he walked toward the center overlook to gaze at the lake.

As he stepped into the overlook, Jeff noticed a smooth surface peeking out from the piles of dried leaves that had gathered where the wall met the ground. Amidst the orange and brown leaves the item stood out like a sore thumb. Taking interest, he carefully brushed aside the dead leaves which crumpled as he did so, to see what it was. To his surprise, what emerged from beneath the leaves was a vandalized garden statue.

The garden statue must have, at some point, depicted a greek goddess of some sort. Wearing only a toga and leaving little to the imagination, the woman's grey form remained intact outside of the crude writing scribbled in white paint. "The White Lady" was painted across the statue in uneven letters, while the face had been systematically smashed off. On top of that, the statue was covered with dirt. Looking down at it, Jeff figured some punk kid must have lifted it from one of the surrounding house's gardens, and brought it to the castle in some strange, ritualistic defiance against the old legend. Strangely, Jeff was comforted by the fact the story was still sticking around enough to lead to this, albeit petty act.

He stooped down and picked up the sad, discarded statue, and placed it upright. Jeff figured it must have been placed there recently, seeing as the base was still smeared brown with fresh mulch. "Sorry about that!" he apologized to either the statue or its owners, he himself wasn't really sure which, then he moved the garden statue so it was sitting on the smooth wall top that acted as a counter. Against the dark backdrop of the sky, the statue seemed ominous, and for the first time since arriving Jeff felt the same tickle of fear he'd felt as a kid.

Instantly, a small spiral notebook appeared from his back pocket. He flipped through until he found an empty page, then began writing: TINGLING, DISMAY, CHOPPY, ATMOSPHERIC, CADAVEROUS, EERIE. Jeff jotted down the words at a machine gun pace, trying to capture any small bit of the moment that he might be able to grab a hold of and use for later. When he finished scribbling he looked up at the statue who, despite not having a face, seemed to be watching him. He tilted his head apologetically, "sorry, gotta strike when the inspiration hits you!" he told the stature, then stuffed the notebook down into his back pocket.

It had gotten dark quickly. The sky was a deep purple, and the lake beneath was even darker; it was only the sound of the crashing waves and slight reflection of the moon and stars that allowed him to still appreciate it. On a whim that he himself didn't understand, Jeff took the notebook back out of his pocket, plopped it on top of the wall and opened it back up, then hoisted himself up until he was sitting on the wall. Beneath his dangling legs was both the wall and the hill beneath, and somewhere in the recesses of his mind he heard the distant voice of little Mikey that afternoon they'd explored the area. *"If you sit on the wall and you're bad, she'll push you right off... my brother sat on it and was fine, but he said another middle schooler in a different class from him died!"* Jeff shook his head and smiled at the long-forgotten memory, and tried to capture some more words as the night set in about him.

Curiosity had transformed to full-fledged interest, and Marisa leaned on the wall and watched the young man. He was talking to himself, occasionally shouting out a word like, "chilling", or, "ancestral", then he'd quickly jot them down in the notebook next to him. Beside him was a strange statue that he'd positioned on the wall, and occasionally he would take a break from writing, look at it, and start up a conversation.

"The atmosphere is just... I don't know, uninspiring. I know what I want to say, and how I want the readers to feel. But how do I explain a place without simply listing off physical attributes. No one wants to read that," he said, his voice brimming with frustration.

Marisa moved closer trying to get a better look at the notebook. When she was about three feet away the young man bristled, suddenly sitting more upright while looking around.

"Must be the breeze..." she heard him mutter. Still, he continued to shift around slightly agitated.

At the same time, the surrounding elm and chestnut trees began to rustle and shake in a similarly flustered state. The whole forest seemed to ripple like a mirage, and she watched as the young man turned around to see what had caused the commotion. Marisa looked back at the young man who began stammering.

"I'm seeing things. Not real. Not real!" he practically shouted over the wind, which had suddenly become a high-pitched wailing that attacked his senses. As the wind whipped about, Jeff watched as the figure grew closer, moving at a steady yet disarming pace. He was watching a scene from a childhood nightmare, his body was a simple passive observer with no agency. He couldn't run, couldn't fight back; he was engulfed by some invisible quicksand. Removed of agency, he was forced to watch the nightmare play out.

The woman, hell, he knew who it was, the White Lady emerged from the trees. There was no translucent glow or slight radiance that he'd come to associate with ghosts from thousands of bad horror movies. No, the woman heading toward him was, if anything, a vacuum to any light that might appear. A black hole devouring any surrounding goodness, draining it like a vampire. She was dressed in a fraying grey dress, which was the same pallid color as a tombstone, while her face was the similarly unnerving grey of a water-logged corpse dragged up from the depths. The dress was made up of heavy material giving it the texture and appearance of a burlap sack as it fluttered behind her.

Behind her, a pair of red eyes glowed and moved throughout the trees. Jeff could see the shadowy silhouette of dogs weaving throughout the foliage, though they remained hidden in the dark. Even above the shrill wind, the sound of their growls cut through and reverberated about Jeff's skull.

He tried to move, but his body betrayed him. Sitting on the edge of the wall instead of peering out over the lake he was frozen in fear, facing the forest and something external, yet equally powerful. Next to him, his notebook fluttered in the wind, the pages blowing back and forth and containing a litany of words he now doubted he would have a chance to use. The childhood fear was no longer a tremor, now it was a full blown earthquake rattling through his being and sending the sirens blaring. "GET OUT AT ONCE" the fruitless warning blared inside, but he was stuck. Beside him, the garden statue rattled on the stone wall until an especially violent gust of wind knocked it over and off the wall. Somewhere several feet below, Jeff heard the sudden crash and explosion of the statue bursting into thousands of pieces.

Marisa watched as the young man grew more horrified. Sweat beaded down his face in tiny droplets, and occasionally he let out a few stings of sentences or words calling for help; but despite all this, he had stayed sitting on the wall with the strange garden statue he'd erected until some unseen force had sent it hurtling off the castle. Marisa, who had paused her approach when he'd first grown agitated returned to slowly creeping forward, still interested in seeing what the notebook said. When she was finally beside him, she quickly placed her hand on the fluttering sheets, and began reading.

The growls grew louder and were now accompanied by the sound of snapping teeth. Even the glowing eyes from the forest seemed to grow in intensity until they were blood red, staring right at Jeff. The White Lady continued toward Jeff, her ragged dress blowing in the wind like the grim reapers. She was now close enough to where Jeff could see her face. Her eyes were the same dark grey as her dress, and a series of long scars ran across her ghastly face. She was more skeleton than human, with skin that seemed to leach into the bones beneath, but it was her eyes that drew Jeff's terrified attention. Like deep wells, they stared back at him with listless emptiness that beckoned for him to be swallowed in their cavernous abyss. *I'm going to die.*

The thought pierced through with perfect clarity, and Jeff, for the first time since the White Lady emerged, relaxed slightly. It was strange that the overwhelming acceptance was calming, but, perhaps in an act of self-preservation, his mind shifted back to the author's lens. He watched her draw close, still unable to move, but wanting to capture everything--futile though it may be. Out of the corner of his eye, Jeff even looked toward his notebook wishing he could write his final thoughts down. The pages were still flipping, but strangely, despite the still roaring wind the pages were turning slowly, methodically, as if someone was reading them...

For the most part, the notebook consisted of a strange and random spatter of words with no clear link or connection. Marisa kept flipping through, trying to understand anything about the young man and why he was here, or why he had this notebook. She looked up at him briefly and saw he was still in a strange state, but that he had relaxed slightly, and went back to reading.

Almost done with the notebook, she was about to give up and head back to the beach to watch the waves and admire the way they reflected the moonlight. She decided to read one last page. She flipped the sheet, realized she had been reading backwards and was actually at the beginning of the notebook, and read the first entry. It was then that she understood. There, scribbled in smudged pencil in giant letters that took up almost the whole sheet was the sentence that finally explained the young man. "Tell the story to understand yourself. Tell your story." Slowly, it all clicked for Marisa. He was a storyteller, a writer.

She was now mere feet away, and despite the teeth-snapping hell hounds and the ancient vengeance-crazed spectre drawing near, the creative juices were flowing. *I could tell the story from her perspective; I could write about a historian researching the legend and finding out about the story; I could write about a bunch of fourth graders who break the curse; I could write about how the legend was initially fake, but manifests itself based on the communal belief... and what about the girl. The poor girl who went missing and started all this? I could write about her dreams, her ambitions cut short and how she too haunts these shores.* Stories and ideas were exploding like fireworks in his cerebellum. *Too bad I'm never going to write them.* In one last act of dedication to his craft before he was surely tossed to his death, Jeff turned to grab the notebook to jot down a final thought. He was still stuck, only his eyes were able to make the turn toward the notebook, which was opened to the first page.

"Tell the story to understand yourself. Tell your story." There it was; the mantra that had gotten him into this whole mess. The core of every piece of fiction writing he'd ever produced. Jeff had jotted it down when he first started writing, trying to find some words or an idea that he could use as fuel for when the journey got tough, or the rejection letters got overwhelming. The why.

Despite the impending doom, Jeff smiled.

Marisa stepped in front of the young man and grabbed his shoulders. She tried talking to him, asking him questions about his writing, and what was his favorite book, and how long he'd been writing... but her questions, whenever posed to passerbys or visitors to the beach, as always, went unanswered. Marisa stopped talking and stared deep into his eyes, trying to find some connection, and then he smiled. She smiled back.

The White Lady stopped two feet in front of the now smiling Jeff. Suddenly, her grey eyes seemed to come alive, as they looked about wildly. Her eyes, those empty pits of despair, grew vibrant and began peering around as she searched for something... or someone. Jeff watched, intrigued by the sudden change. She looked about and suddenly, the wind died down. Then, the growling stopped and the glowing red eyes disappeared from the trees. Lastly, and within seconds, the White Lady was gone, vanished into thin air.

Immediately Jeff's bodily control returned, and he leaped off the wall in a sudden burst. As soon as his feet touched the ground he was off running; but halfway down the steps, he stopped. *The notebook.* It took every ounce of will to overpower the drive to get the hell out of there and never look back, but he managed to retrace his steps and return to the wall to retrieve the notebook. When he arrived it was still open, but rather than being on the first page, the journal was flipped to where he'd left off. There, in elegant handwriting much too pretty to be his own, was a note:

"Tell my story too- Marisa"

Marisa watched as the young man disappeared, holding the notebook close to his chest and no longer running. Instead, he walked down the steps slowly, with a starry-eyed gaze across his face. She smiled, confident her story was in the right hands, and followed down the steps back toward the beach. Back to where the moon reflected on Lake Ontario just right, and back to where she was free to wonder and be curious for all time.

LULLABY OF HIGHBANK BRIDGE

by Jen Sexton-Riley

This story starts with a wild, swirling night. No, no, no. Not the dark and stormy kind. It isn't that sort of story at all. Not that sort of night. We're talking the kind of New England seaside night made of warm June air thickened with marine fog, the kind of night with clouds full of moonlight. The kind of night that feels heavy with story.

Coco opens the door and steps out into the humid salt air. She doesn't notice the story hanging in it. Coco whirls left and right on the front stairs of the apartment house. She runs down the steps to the sandy front path and pauses, again looking right, again looking left. Marisa is gone.

Marisa has been having a rough time lately. She's been distant. At the table she stares off through the walls into an unknown distance. In bed she is cool, reserved, except when she startles out of nightmares with a gasp, as if rising from the bottom of some solitary depth that has almost drowned her. Lately it is only at these vulnerable times in the haze between dream and awareness that Coco feels close to Marisa again. Holding her, trembling, in the darkness, as it used to be. Marisa doesn't tell her about the nightmares. Coco is afraid to ask. Afraid that Marisa won't answer, and that the membrane of silence will rise again between them, insinuating itself in the space between even as Coco cradles Marisa, two spoons fitting together in perfect curves.

The full moon slides in and out of view behind fast moving clouds, painting Coco's strained features pale and then dark. She's called Marisa's phone more times than seems reasonable. She's left cool, casual voicemails. She's left anxious voicemails. She's texted. Marisa doesn't have any friends to check in with, at least none Coco knows about. She's been cagey about friends. She's been cagey about introducing Coco to her family too, so there's no help there. Several places come to mind in flashes. Where can she be?

It's a quick walk south to twisting Highbank Road, then a left turn to the river, to the bridge. Marisa is prone to moody walks. The mid-span vantage point above the swirling salty waters of Bass River, which changes direction with the changing tides, is a common destination. If not for a few old riverbank houses in the way and oaks in full summer leaf, Coco would have a clear view of Marisa on the bridge. If she's there.

Coco is jogging down the red brick sidewalk before she realizes she's doing it, visualizing Marisa at the waist, over the old's bridges south side barrier wall, chin resting on folded arms on the rough, stony surface. As she reaches the Highbank intersection and turns left toward the river, the figure of Marisa, in exactly the pose Coco imagined, layers itself neatly over the version in her imagination. Coco inhales a chestful of the sea-heavy river air--realizing she's been holding her breath--and slows to a walk, willing her feet to silence.

Marisa stands motionless, staring down into the river.

As she draws closer, Coco notices a shape on the other side of the bridge. A figure. A stranger is watching Marisa from the shadows. He seems to be singing a soft tune that Coco knows, but she can't quite place it before the wind snatches it away from her ears. Coco thinks she hears his song, or feels it somehow, gently willing Marisa to jump. Coco goes to her, touches her shoulder, her fingers stroking the familiar soft texture of her jacket.

The touch seems to shake Marisa out of a stupor. Her breath quickens, yet she still stares down into the river. Coco follows her gaze into the deep roiling green, hints of the pale river bottom winking below, echoing the moonlight. Coco searches the shadows across the bridge for the man. There is no one there. They turn away from the river and head for home. "Who was that man?" Coco asks, matching Marisa's strides. Left. Right. Together. "I could have sworn I heard him telling you to jump. In a song?"

Marisa winces away, curling her chin down near her shoulder, away from Coco's pleading eyes.

"What man," she replies. Like a statement. Flat.

Flashback. Spring. When they met it felt to Coco like she'd happened upon another of her species for the first time. She finally felt seen. Understood. Marisa was right here in the moment with Coco, not constantly looking backward, obsessing about some past that was gone forever, asking a lot of questions without answers or straining to see an unseeable future, worrying and trying to prepare for things that may never happen. Everything was right here and now for Marisa and Coco. They encountered the world and each other as if they were brand new, and what better season than spring to discover everything together? Icicles were still melting from the eaves of the apartment house with its weathered grey shingles when Coco first took Marisa home. The little peeper frogs sang them to sleep that first night. Their first morning was like the very first morning of all, awash with crocuses piercing through a final spring melt. Lavender, daffodils, snowdrops and hellebore wriggle and unfurled their faces to the first early warblers and the lingering chickadees, the sighing treble of blackbirds and the sleepy catbirds' mew. Coco rose and Coco shone. Their hands, their appetites, even their shoes were the same size, and Marisa didn't ask what had happened to Coco's little toe. She just counted them off--one, two, three, four--and that was that.

But spring turns to summer, and the pale morning light becomes oppressive. Stone becomes too hot to touch. By June Marisa had turned her face away, listening to a song Coco couldn't hear. The daily things of life now seem like too much bother, too complicated, too much fuss for Marisa. Coco feels less and less like part of a happily matched pair and more like an interruption. A disruption. She used to delight and mystify Marisa. Now she drives her away. To the bridge. To the river. To the water which she wouldn't touch.

Marisa hated the water. She refused to swim. It was the first time something hadn't surprised and delighted her. She curled her lip back in a snarl. Now her face is cool and expressionless and she is drawn to the swirl of the river, but never in daylight. Only in darkness, with the full moon glinting across the complexities of the changing currents. Do people die by jumping from bridges into rivers? Coco checks the news for stories of drownings, of bodies, finds nothing. She wishes she could call someone. Coco doesn't remember her mother. She never knew her father. It's all a blur, as if it happened to someone else. There's only Marisa, and then the empty space where Marisa used to be. And the river.

They're arguing. Marisa is always overwhelmed. Always closing her eyes. Blocking out the too muchness of life. Too many things are happening, she says.

"Like what?" Coco says.

"Like all of *this*," she says, gesturing.

Coco looks around the room wildly. They are sitting in the silent living room, lights turned low. Coco has been reading a book while Marisa stares into the distance through the wall.

Coco doesn't even try to listen to music anymore. Everything is too much. Too too much. Coco wants to make friends. To create a life. People have friends and lives. Holidays and nights out. Movies. People go to the movies with friends. Coco knows this because she's seen it happen in movies. Marisa is silent. She sits at attention and closes her eyes.

Does she have a secret? Some weird past? What if she isn't who she says she is? What if she is secretly--Coco whirls through possibilities in her mind--a spy? A runaway? Is she married? Has she committed a crime? Coco remembers their first morning together when Marisa first noticed her missing toe in the early spring sunlight. Coco tried to hide it. But Marisa pulled the blanket aside and saw the empty space and it didn't matter. Not one bit. Marisa seemed to grow to love Coco's flaw, staring at the place where the toe should be. Where is Marisa now? She's gone again. She was just here. She was sitting *right there*. Coco pulls back the curtain and notices a strange man standing in the moonlight looking up at the house. His lips are moving slowly, as if he is reciting something. Or singing. He is leaning on some sort of wheeled cart, a dolly. Then the moon slides under a cloud and he is gone.

When things go sideways between couples in movies, sometimes the one who is more in love--because there's always one who is more in love, tries to find a way back to the way things were. Coco takes Marisa for a walk in the park by the river in the early morning, when the sun hasn't quite reached its full power and the morning feels cool and new, a little bit like spring. It's so early that no cars are on the streets, and only a few people are fishing on the riverbank, one of them somewhat surreally dressed in a suit and tie. Coco and Marisa gravitate without speaking toward the fountain in the center of the park, a shallow pool within a low stone wall, with the stone figure of a young woman dancing on a pedestal at its center. They stare at the pale stone figure, its face turned up and frozen in a carefree smile, unblinking stone eyes wide in the unrelenting spill of the fountain's spray. Coco stands motionless beside Marisa for a long time before gently moving her hand closer, closer to Marisa's until their hands touch. Marisa closes her eyes and relaxes her hand, allowing Coco to wind their fingers together. Marisa sighs. Softens. Her fingers become warm. She says she will try harder. Coco's eyes fill with hot tears. She blinks them away to avoid overwhelming Marisa again and ruining the moment. Her throat aches with the effort.

Maybe everything will be okay.

Coco is arriving home with bags of groceries when she notices the landlady, Mrs. Gould, weeding her flower bed around the base of a new statue.

"I bought it from the strangest man last night," Mrs. Gould says in a low voice, almost whispering. "I saw him going down the street with it on a dolly, singing. He said he's a sculptor. Or...a gardener? Anyway, he has a studio, or a garden, something, on the other side of the river, just across the bridge. The old salt works building. I didn't even know there was anyone using that building, let alone an artist! And *what* an artist. What talent! Why, I wouldn't be a bit surprised if she opened her eyes and spoke. And he practically gave it to me for a song--"

Marisa arrives home at that moment from one of her long walks, coming around the corner and into the garden. She looks up, startled, sees the statue and stops in her tracks. Her eyes growing wide, she inhales deeply and screams, her knees nearly buckling with the violence of it. Coco runs to her side and throws her arms around Marisa's shoulders, half steering and half carrying her into the house.

After an hour of being held tightly as she trembles and sobs, Marisa's breaths have calmed and deepened. She is asleep. Coco slips away and discovers a note that Mrs. Gould has slipped under the door. She hopes that Coco's "friend" is feeling better, and would like to remind Coco that this is in fact a one-bedroom rental, meant for one tenant only. Marisa's nocturnal comings and goings are just too weird, and this screaming episode has spooked the other tenants. They've been good, reliable renters and she doesn't want to lose them, so she hopes Coco will let her know when her "guest" will be leaving, or else the two of them will just have to find a new place to live. A two-bedroom rental someplace, that would make more sense, wouldn't it?

Coco is dreading telling Marisa. When she eventually does, Marisa goes flat, cold and motionless. She knew this would happen. She just can't move with the changes. She runs out of the house.

Now Coco can't find Marisa anywhere. She doesn't answer her phone. She's not home. Her usual spot on the bridge is empty. The idea that she might have walked to the fountain at the park where they had their hopeful moment was nothing but a bit of wishful romantic fantasy. She was nowhere. It's starting to get dark, and Coco is on the verge of panic. On the way back home she checks the bridge one more time and sees the strange man, the one who seemed to sing that odd, familiar song to Marisa all those nights ago. He is pulling something out of the river. A garden statue. It glows in the moonlight, dripping wet. The man throws a length of burlap over it and secures it to a dolly, walks away singing his strange song, like a lullaby. Coco is drawn by the sound.

Coco follows him, keeping to the shadows and only crossing the bridge when he has gone far enough ahead. The man's hair is a brilliant white in the moonlight, yet he moves, with too much limber grace. Like a much younger man. The ease with which he maneuvers the life-sized stone figure, which must weigh hundreds of pounds, is not what she expects from someone of his years. At worst, she fears that what she is seeing is impossible. Even a healthy young man--maybe several--would struggle to move the statue.

After a few twists and turns down smaller and smaller lanes, the man moves the statue through a wrought iron gate covered with ivy into the old salt works property, which seems to have been transformed into a strange garden filled with statues. He pauses, fumbles through a great number of keys on a ring and then unlocks a door and steps into the building's dark interior, leaving Coco alone with the statue. Emboldened by the sound of his song deep within the building, Coco steps out of the shadows toward the covered statue. The distant music seems to lift her arm and close her fingers around the rough texture of the burlap fabric. As the distant song falls silent and the moon emerges from behind a cloud, Coco pulls the burlap off the statue. Marisa's face glows in the moonlight, smooth and cold. Any trace of her usual troubled expression is gone. She looks serene. Relieved.

"Where is she? What have you done with her?"

Coco screams into the dark building, no longer afraid of being discovered.

"I saw you! I heard your little song. You were telling her to jump off the bridge! I know you were!"

In the lightless interior of the salt works building, the man's footsteps approach and then stop. Coco strains her eyes in the darkness but can't see anything. She hears the soft sound of a chain being grasped and pulled, and the light of a single bulb illuminates the enormous room. Coco gasps. Arranged everywhere are life sized sculptures of people, women and men in various positions. They are all as lifelike and expressive as the sculpture of Marisa, each face as serene and untroubled as Marisa's smooth features. They look as if they might at any moment breathe, speak, move.

Coco forces herself to look away from the smooth stone faces and into the eyes of the white-haired man. His eyes are intense, but soft. His face wears an expression that she can't quite define. It isn't unkind, but there is an odd, silent laughter playing across his features.

"I wasn't telling her to jump, Coco," he says calmly. His tone reminds Coco of a lion tamer in a movie, coaxing a wild beast back into its cage. "I was inviting her. The moonlight. The river. And yes, my song. It was an invitation. It was..." He steps closer to Coco, holding onto the doorframe to steady herself. "It was a kindness."

"A kindness? I don't--I don't understand. How do you know my name? Where is--" Coco turns to look at the sculpture of Marisa behind her in the moonlight, and she knows. It isn't a sculpture of Marisa.

"You know where she is. She is-- there," the man says gently, gesturing to Marisa with a weathered hand. "I knew you would be different, Coco. Because of this." He reaches into his collar and reveals a chain hanging around his neck. Something small and curved hangs from it, something that shines in the moonlight.

"My... toe?" Coco gasps. The room begins to spin. Pale faces of smooth stone, their eyes wide and blank, their lips soft and bland curves of peace, swirl past as she sits heavily on the floor.

"Yes, your toe! I didn't know how it would affect you, but somehow having this--this little missing piece seems to have made you better able to deal with the slings and arrows of human existence, if you will. This little... I don't want to call it a flaw, but this tiny difference somehow enables you, Coco, to succeed where all the rest of my creations fail. They all come looking for the way home, some sooner and some later. They all come to my little lullaby on the bridge and they reach for the moonlight on the river. All except you."

The bright glare of the light bulb continues to spin as Coco wilts the rest of the way onto the floor.

"Someday maybe you'll understand," the man says as darkness closes over her head and she loses consciousness. "Someday you too may crave such a kindness."

Coco wakes up alone in her bed. It is the middle of the afternoon. Her room is filled with summer sunshine. Her head throbs.

She considers calling the police, but what can she say? None of it makes any sense. She looks down into the apartment house's courtyard garden and hears the strange song in the distance. Is it a memory? Mrs. Gould's new garden statue slowly lifts her chin and a slow smile spreads across its face. Coco closes her eyes and imagines walking to Marisa's place on the bridge. She hears the song in the distance growing louder. She hears a splash.

Coco wakes up. Mrs. Gould is shaking her.

"Are you okay?" Mrs. Gould says. Her watering can splashes Coco's face. She realizes she has been asleep on the garden bench.

"Yes, I'm okay. I'm so sorry. I was out searching for Marisa so late, I must have fallen asleep. I think she's left and she isn't coming back."

"Well, what a coincidence. My new garden statue is gone too. If you ever hear from her again, you let her know I want my statue back. That's theft, and I won't tolerate it. I knew there was something off about that young woman." Mrs. Gould scowls, then smiles in exasperation. "Let's get you inside, you poor thing. She's done a number on us both."

Coco lies in bed remembering. If she chooses to go on with her life, it is with the knowledge that she isn't really a person like everyone else. Marisa chose to be made of stone rather than face the unknowns, the fears and uncertainties of life. Coco has to accept that. And she has to accept that whatever it is in her that allows her to adapt and go on is, in a way, monstrous. She pulls back the blanket and looks at the empty place where her toe should be.

She often sees men and women standing on the bridge, staring down the water. She sometimes hears the lullaby. Sometimes it calls to her. Someday it will be too strong. She closes her eyes and imagines her nine toes plunging into the silty bottom, the sand rushing to kiss her knees, the water closing over her head and drowning the moonlight. Someday she will accept that kindness. She imagines it would be good to have Marisa here, standing in the garden, or in the corner of the bedroom, her smooth, mild face a lifelike expression of curiosity, of openness, the way she was in spring, in the beginning of the story. Before it all became too much and it was all too hot and the call of moonlight on the river was so cool and her face closed into stone and then-- and then.

For now, although this story ends, Coco continues to live. It isn't exactly a happily ever after kind of story, but no one dissolves into tears and sea foam either. Nobody gets roasted by witches or gobbled by wolves. No one is tricked into eating a poisoned apple. Marisa remains still and untroubled in her garden of stone across the Highbank Bridge. Coco, on her side of the river, holds onto another Marisa in the tower of her memory, the springtime Marisa, twirling and smiling, forever warm and alive. Coco smiles and holds her aloft, far above the river and the garden, protecting her with the patience and cold detachment of stone.

ROAD FLARES

By Neil Willoughby

The practice of willingly eating dirt is called *Geophagy*. I learned about this last semester in my AP Humanities course.

Despite the lack of scientific evidence, many cultures believe that ingesting soil has a vast array of health benefits- from altering skin tone to alleviating morning sickness. A diagnosable mental illness, *Pica*, is an eating disorder based on cravings for non-food items. Some people suffering from *Pica* feel an insatiable urge to eat dirt. Unfortunately, at least to my knowledge, there is no specific term for the sensation of pure horror as dirt forces itself down your throat- a consequence of being buried alive.

I may not have the proper terminology, but I can tell you what it feels like: road flares. The kind emergency services use on the highway to direct traffic away from a collision. They burn with a slow ferocity, illuminating the very terrors they are intended to divert you from, leaving a ghost of cinders in their wake. Embers and ash; scorching my throat and igniting my lungs as I feverishly start to dig.

"Marisa, come get some breakfast!" my dad bellows upstairs from the kitchen. The scent of pancake batter and sizzling bacon lazily wafts into my room, but I fail to notice it in my developing panic.

"One sec Dad, I'm still getting ready!" I yell back. The zipper is catching on the dress he bought me for today. The elegant sea-foam green sheath dress was a little bright for my taste, and I knew it was WAY out of our price range, but Dad made me try it on at the department store on the rich side of the mall. When I came out of the changing stall to show him, I could see his eyes start to well.

"Your eyes, you look like- ", he said swallowing back his tears.

"Is this the one then?" I asked quickly, offering him a half-smile and successfully dodging the conversation he was about to start.

He nodded softly.

Don't get me wrong, besides my battle with the zipper, I actually like the dress. It has a nice half sleeve that makes me a little less self-conscious about my arms and it's flowy- but it still has a shape. And I guess my Dad was right, there is something to be said about the contrast of this light green against my dark, chestnut-colored eyes.

Emerging victorious against my formidable, jagged-toothed enemy, I grab my black Dr. Marten boots and hastily shove my feet in.

"Marisa, you okay up there?" he calls again. I know he's worried about today- so am I.

Today is the Annual Grayson Estate Women's Society Afternoon Tea. Something my mom's family puts on every year where all the *distinguished ladies* and their spoiled daughters gather around to brag about which Ivy league university they're going to attend and what profession their future *husband* is in. All while sipping leaf juice and gazing upon, but never really partaking in, a plethora of carefully arranged hors d'oeuvres and finger sandwiches. Mom never liked going, and either did I, but it was insisted upon both of us. This year, I have to go alone.

I grab my bag off my bed, toss in the sensible, pink lipstick I just applied, the book I'm reading for AP Literature (Vonnegut's *Slaughterhouse Five*), and shut the door on my way downstairs.

Dad is sitting down at the table as I enter the kitchen and he beams at me in delight- at least until he sees my boots.

"Are you sure you want to wear those today?" he asks with a slight frown, "You know how these people are…"

"I am sure." I say confidently, "For me, they *spark joy.*" I smirk at him, quoting one of the self-help methods he has been trying to utilize, in an effort to bring some sense of normalcy to our lives.

"Ok then. You feeling comfortable is the most important thing today," he conceded, "And if you want to leave early, I'll stay close at a coffee shop in town and grade some papers."

"To be fair, I don't want to go at all" I half-joke.

He sighs and looks down in dismay at the half-eaten pancake in front of him. He's not necessarily a prideful man, but we both know he won't be able to help me financially for university next year on his modest, community-college professor's salary.

"But I get that it is a necessary evil," I continued, "and as out of touch and, um, let's say *conservative* as they are- they are family- I guess."

Dad looked back at me, his eyes clearly thankful that I hadn't made him acknowledge the harsh truth of the situation that we both understood. Mom's family never liked Dad- as he was not from the societal elites they preferred to keep company with. Dad was working part-time as a teacher's assistant while he was getting his master's degree when they met, and Mom was a student in the class. They were only two and a half years apart, but Mom's family affluence afforded her the opportunity to travel abroad for a year or so before starting classes. They bonded over a paper he helped her write analyzing Kahlil Gibran's, "*The Prophet*". After talking through the chapter "*on love*", they were in it. And although Mom never spoke poorly of her family, she always insisted (especially after gatherings like the one today) that we were just "cut from a different cloth than the rest of her family", and in a lot of ways, she thought that was a good thing.

After the accident, it *wasn't* a good thing though. At her funeral, the family kept my Dad at arm's-length, barely acknowledging the sorrow of the man she had spent the last twenty years with. Instead of sending well wishes in the following weeks, he received calls from their lawyers. They allowed him to cash in a meager life insurance policy and gave nothing more than their word that I would be taken care of.

So, I had to go today. Otherwise, it was a simple case of "out of sight, out of mind" and my chances at retaining some of the privilege of their family's money, well *technically* my family's money, would be lost and I know Dad didn't want that.

I hastily wolfed down a couple pancakes at the kitchen island and grabbed my water bottle from the fridge.

"Welp, might as well get on the road now in case there's any traffic", I suggested half-heartedly. It was an hour and a half drive to the Grayson Estate. Most of it was scenic countryside, with picturesque, rolling hills and horse-filled valleys, but just off the highway- about fifteen minutes from the estate- was a heavily wooded two track dirt road that connected the interstate to a small downtown nearby. This patch of winding road was almost intolerable to navigate after dark, and the thick fog on the night of the accident didn't help.

After a little over an hour of Dad and I poorly crooning some of his favorite oldies together, we pulled off the interstate and onto the dirt road. I clutched the bag in my lap, white-knuckling it through the sharp twists and turns. Dad was driving cautiously, and he noticed how distraught I was. He put a hand on my shoulder, trying to help relax me.

"Both hands on the wheel please!" I snapped.

He sullenly complied. "Dad, I'm sorry, I just.."

"No, no- I understand." He assured me.

As we passed through the exact stretch of road where it happened, the memory was palpable. The smoke and twisted steel. Rich oil spilling into the black dirt. The hood of the little powder blue Prius crumpled into its dashboard and the copper- tainted scent of blood. The sirens and the lights. The road flares. I caught a glimpse of her arm, idly hanging out of the driver's side window, cast in the blazing orange light. That's when Dad spun me around by my shoulders and ordered me to look away, to look at the ground, to look at anything besides the inescapable horrors in front of me. I was in shock, too stunned to defy his command. I silently watched the road flares burn, each slowly revealing a line of hot white ash, dreading when the light would go out.

"Marisa? Hey, Marisa, just breathe," his voice pulled me out of the waking nightmare. I had inadvertently been holding my breath, and took a few startled gasps before I was leveled enough to reply.

"Maybe this isn't a good idea right now. I didn't want to pressure you- ", he started to say, but I cut him off before he could finish.

"I'm fine. It's okay, *really*."

He didn't seem convinced in the least, but he kept driving.

We arrived at the massive iron gates, marked with a crest bearing the words "Le phénix" under an intricately engraved representation of the mythical fowl. There was an old story passed down in the family, some lore about their great, great grandfather catching a phoenix and striking a deal to release it, in exchange for some of its magic. The fable was meant to aggrandize the inherent cunning of their bloodline and offered a fun anecdote to explain the wealth that had not truly been earned by the last few generations.

The gates hummed as the motorized chains slowly opened them. Dad's Honda Civic crawled up the quarter-mile drive and into the half circle at the entrance to the manor.

"Are you sure you're okay?" he asked.

"I'll be fine- it's nothing I haven't dealt with before. I love you, Dad. I'll see you in a few hours."

"I love you too."

I gave him a quick hug and swung open the car door to hop out, clutching my bag and adjusting my dress. I waved as he turned around and departed back down the drive. As I started to head toward the manor, an older tuxedoed man with a neatly trimmed, gray mustache signaled to me from the path at the side of the house.

"Ah, Miss Marisa. I'm so glad you could join us!" the syrupy-sweetness of his words oozed with phony affection.

"Glad to be here, Robert."

"May I take your bag, *mademoiselle?*"

"No, I think I'm going to hold onto it today, I may do some reading in the gardens later."

"Mm-hmm," his façade slipped with a tight-lipped attempt at a smile that read more like a sneer, "please follow me around to the courtyard in the gardens."

The Grayson Estate has a sprawling, bountiful garden across two acres. The back two-thirds are covered by a labyrinth of ten-foot tall, expertly manicured hedges that encompass what the designer calls a "jardin à la française". Fantastical floral designs that simultaneously boast the power of nature and defy its' laws- are woven into the maze, accentuating the tasteful fountains and statuaries that pay tribute to the legacy that funded their creation. At the mouth of this Eden is a slightly raised plateau that supports a pristine white marble patio, allowing a vantage point to appreciate the vast complexity of the topiaries surrounding it.

The patio itself was home to a massive marble table that could easily seat fifty guests. For today's festivities, each place was set with lavender cloth napkins and brilliant ivory plates, lined with what was sure to be solid gold. As Robert led me up the small staircase onto patio, I could feel my hands starting to sweat with nervous anticipation.

"Madame Claudette, I present to you Mademoiselle Marisa", Robert's voice bellowed through the crowded table of ladies.

"Hi Grandma", I said with as much of a smile as I could muster.

"Oh, ma belle petit-fille!" Claudette gushed as she rose from her seat at the head of the table, revealing a high neck A- line dress that matched the lavender of the napkins, "Come here, I've saved a spot just for you." Her effervescent pearls danced in the sun as she beckoned me toward her.

I could feel the eyes bore into me as I crossed the length of the table. There were whispers, low enough that I couldn't quite make out what they were saying, though it wasn't a stretch of the imagination to guess. Claudette pulled me in close for a long embrace and gestured to a chair on her right. I took a seat, quietly mortified at being thrust into the spotlight. Mom and I were *never* sat anywhere near the head of the table. Those chairs were reserved for either people Claudette was trying to impress, or more likely, people who were trying to impress her.

The staff came around, delicately filling each hand-painted teacup from their sterling silver carafes. The herbal tea reeked of fresh sown earth- quite unpleasantly- at least to my *proletarian* sensitivities. It had to be pushing ninety degrees outside, why in holy hell were we drinking hot tea? I've never understood tradition for tradition's-sake. *Cut from a different cloth*, I guess.

Claudette introduced me to the other ladies surrounding her at the table, most I had already met before.

"This is my granddaughter, Marisa. She's *Elizabeth's* girl." Her voice lowered when she spoke my mother's name, and her eyes sulked in what I must believe to be some sort of genuine grief for her late daughter. The women all stared at me with pitying glances as I squirmed in my seat.

"What happened was a terrible tragedy," Claudette continued, and the entire table hushed, "I miss my daughter, dearly. In times like these, it helps to be surrounded by the family and friends whom I cherish." The women softly smiled with reserved admiration for the matriarch of the Grayson family.

"But today is not a day to mourn, it is a day of celebration! Today we celebrate the wonderful women of our great families. We celebrate all that we have achieved and all we are striving toward. À votre santé!"

"À votre santé!" the women replied in unison.

With that, the table came alive with women chatting- I was

caught in the crossfire of voices trying desperately to reach Claudette's ear. When she responded to one woman around her own age, who I recognized to be the matriarch of another family they were close with, the ladies broke off into side conversations while they politely waited. I offered my Grandmother a smile when she looked over in my direction but was quite keen to remain separate from any prying conversation.

The staff filed in again, this time with sterling silver platters and presented them on all ends of the table. Mounds of petite sandwiches and artisanal pastries were piled on trays, stacked creatively in superb presentation. I spotted my Aunt Lydia and her daughter, Florence, seated near the opposite end of the table. Lydia and my mom never really got along; I think she was envious of the respect Claudette had shown for my mother. Even when they were not on speaking terms, there was a mutual, quiet reverence. Claudette and Lydia never fought like that, but it was clear that Claudette held my mother in higher regard. Lydia and Florence kept shooting furtive glances in my direction, talking energetically to a few of the women around them. I met Florence's gaze on one occasion and gave her a smug little wave. Her brow furrowed in obvious disdain as she swiftly turned away.

After an hour of passively listening to the bile that was considered "polite conversation", my lip was starting to bleed from how hard I was biting it.

"Are you ready?" Claudette leaned over to me. "For what?" I asked.

"Ladies, if you would all please follow me to the entrance of the *jardin à la française*. My daughter, Lydia, has prepared a short speech for the unveiling." Claudette rose and smiled at me. She took my arm, and we ascended the ramp down to the mouth of the hedges behind us.

There was an ornate gold and silver tapestry, embroidered with *Le phénix*, suspended from ground level to a set of poles about seven feet tall. Lydia passed us and flashed Claudette a quick smile, before taking her place in front of the curtain.

"Ladies, thank you all so much for being here today. As my mother so eloquently said earlier, today is a day for celebration. A few months ago, she came to me with the request that I head the design of a tribute to my late sister for the garden."

My stomach sank as a wave of nausea crashed over me.

"I miss my sister every day and my daughter, Florence, had such a special bond with her Aunt Elizabeth. This loss has taken a great toll on *our* family." She feigned a low sob and threw a hand over her face in anguish. Once she composed herself, she continued, "When presented this wonderful opportunity to help celebrate someone so beloved to us, we were honored with the task."

Bullshit. I could feel my face growing hot.

"So without further ado, here is our tribute to my sister, Elizabeth Carol Grayson." With that, Lydia gently pulled a tasseled cord that drew the tapestry aside.

I don't know what I had expected, but there she was. A near perfect representation of my mom, standing with her hands gently clasped in front of her at her waist, staring back at the crowd, cast in polished bronze. I felt hot tears starting to rise. All around her, for about five feet in every direction, tulips were planted of every color. There was no denying their simple beauty, but I knew it was a message. Mom was allergic to tulips, an affliction I had inherited. The base of the statue read:

Elizabeth Carol Grayson: Beloved Daughter and Sister

That wasn't her name. She had been Elizabeth Carol Williams for the past twenty years, a name she shared with my dad and eventually with me. *Beloved Daughter and Sister-* no mention of her last sixteen years as a mother. There was polite applause rising all around me, and some of the women had started lining up to praise Lydia for her work. I couldn't stand to endure another second of it.

I took long, quick strides toward the mouth of the hedges.

There is no way I was going to allow myself to graciously be a part of the commendation for a work that erased *my* family.

"Marisa, where are you running off to?" Claudette shouted after me. I ignored her, feeling the torrid gaze of the women's eyes on my back as I entered the labyrinth and slipped out of sight.

Though I had traversed this maze many times before with my mom, I had no idea which

direction I was headed. When I was far enough away that the voices subsided, I sat down against one of the topiaries. The tears that had been building breached the levees of my anger and I quietly wept into my palms. A few moments later, I started to hear voices again.

"Where the hell is she?" Lydia's voice spat.

"She can't have gone far, and the only way out of here is the way we came in." Robert reminded her. The voices were getting closer.

"This is all your fault, Robert. If you were in the least bit competent, it would have been her father that collided with that tree-"

"Hush your mouth. Now." Claudette commandingly cut her off, "Your idiocy never fails to surprise me."

The trio was about to round the corner to where I was seated. I grabbed my bag and took off sprinting in the other direction. *It was them?* The night of the accident, my dad had to teach a late class, so he met us at the Grayson Estate in time for after-dinner coffee and desserts. When we left that evening, I rode with him. Mom followed behind us- until we had to stop into town to get gas and she drove ahead.

"SHE WENT THIS WAY!" I heard Robert shout as their footsteps gave chase. I darted through zig-zags of lush green walls, dodging all manner of foliage with what could almost be mistaken as grace- that is, until I turned a sharp corner and caught my foot on a raised root that sent me toppling forward into a freshly dug pit. My head slammed hard against the jagged rocks at its base. Dazed, I could just barely make out the shape of three figures standing a few feet above me. Then the lights went out.

When I woke, I gasped, and soil forced its way into my open mouth. I sputtered and spat away as much as I could, but it was already burning me from the inside. I couldn't move- the immense weight of the earth around me left me completely immobilized. I panicked in the pitch black and tried treading through the soil with every ounce of strength I possessed, kicking and punching in every direction, but barely moved. There was a small gap underneath my nostrils, but I couldn't be certain how long that would sustain me.

Attempting to calm myself down, taking short, shallow breaths- I started to dig my right hand toward my mouth- clawing through the rocks and soil. I was making progress when the realization hit me, inducing a fresh terror. How far down was I? I could not recall how deep the pit was, three feet? Six? I had no answer. My thoughts were interrupted by the sensation of something winding itself around my left ankle.

Whatever this creature was, I felt it slither its way up to my mid-thigh, and then ensnare my other ankle soon after. The creature's grip tightened, and I felt its rough, serrated exterior piercing into my skin. I screamed through pursed lips as its tentacles grabbed hold of each or my arms, eliminating the progress I had made with my right hand. The beast started yanking at my limbs, and my head shifted in the ground. Before I could process what was happening, both my nostrils and mouth were filled with earth once again. I instinctively inhaled, searing my insides. I coughed and choked on the dirt involuntarily gasping- drowning myself in the garden.

Suddenly the monster's limbs pulled again- I was moving. Dirt shifted around my body, but without immediate oxygen, I would die before I faced my captor. My brain felt like it was on fire, but soon the sensation started to fade. Being dragged through the rocky earth now felt like floating, and then I saw the flare.

My face broke the topsoil and I was staring into the smoldering sunset above the garden. I was gently set upright, as I hacked dirt up out of my chest. After catching my breath, I looked up to see a beautiful cast bronze representation of *"Le phénix"* woven into the garden wall before me. I saw my distorted reflection in its feathered chest, bruised and broken, but alive. *Risen.* I felt the creature's tentacles release my legs, and quickly looked back to see four thick roots jutting up from the ground, swaying gently. I could not begin to explain why, but I know they were somehow looking at me.

"I need to get out of here." I said softly, mostly to myself. Talking hurt, but apparently it was enough. The roots slid down to the ground, creeping along the path to my left. I followed. They led me through the maze, gaining numbers along the way. When we reached the entrance, they all but filled the sides of the hedges. I stopped in the gaping mouth of the *jardin à la française.*

The women were gathered again, gossiping away on the patio.

I scanned the crowd until I saw *them.* Roger, Lydia, and Claudette were quietly meeting in a corner, away from the guests. Florence was standing a few feet away from her mother, staring intently at her phone. I looked to my left and saw my mother watching them too, through her bronzed eyes.

Rage rapidly came to a boil beneath my skin. I could feel its electricity crackling around me. The foliage must have been able to sense it too- as the army of roots dug their way into the ground in front of me. Unadulterated fury blurred my vision- I wanted them to pay. Not for college, not for a better life for Dad and I, but with their blood.

The ground began to rumble around the raised patio. Expensive china and silver rattled off the table's edge shattering and clanging on the marble floor. Guests screamed and flocked toward the front staircase. Claudette, Robert, Lydia, and Florence had shakily crossed to the table when the marble began to crack beneath them. From the blooming crevasse, heavy vines and roots began to emerge. The divide opened wider, swallowing the enormous marble table whole.

Guests were scrambling across the yard toward the manor. Anguished shrieks filled the air as the horde trampled over one another to safety. The shaking ground had sent Claudette to her knees and Robert rushed to her aide. Lydia grabbed Florence's arm and tried to make a mad dash on the uneven ground toward the crumbling staircase. Neither of them noticed the chasm expanding when Florence's foot landed on the edge. Her body jerked toward the bottomless expanse and she clawed at her mother to catch her. Instead, Lydia released Florence's arm and shrunk back as she watched her daughter tumble into the earth.

Lydia hesitated a moment before continuing her sprint toward salvation. She was within five feet of the staircase when one of the tentacle arms caught her around the midsection and pulled her up into air above the canyon. Vines had crept behind Robert and Claudette as well, slowly circling their prey. I took a few steps toward the chaos and gazed in wonder at the eldritch horror I had unleashed.

"Marisa, help us!" Claudette pleaded to me as the roots and vines ensnared her and Robert.

The monstrosity set Lydia down next to them, keeping a tight grasp on her. Looking into their eyes, I could still see the disgust behind their fear. The vines and roots gripped tighter. Their eyes bulged and faces turned blue as they tried to struggle free. I looked over again at the sculpture of my mom, pleasantly smiling back at me. As I turned back to the trio responsible for her death, I clenched my fists and the vegetation slowly began crushing them. Gore spewed from their fragile bodies, spattering my torn dress. The greenery started retreating into the crevasse, dragging the deflated remains with it. The ground began quaking harder as the whole plateau collapsed into the pit, leaving a giant sinkhole in the middle of the Grayson Estate. Then, it was calm.

I stumbled over to the guests gathered at the manor. About

halfway there, someone spotted me and a couple of them came running. Sirens were blaring beyond the gate as the first responders arrived. As soon as the two ladies helped me to the circle drive, I collapsed on pavement.

EMTs rushed over and carried me to the back of an ambulance to assess my wounds.

"Is she going to be alright?" I heard the grave concern in his voice.

"I'm good, Dad." I mumbled through the oxygen mask they had strapped to my head.

"What happened?! I was in town and saw the sirens heading this way- so I just hopped in the car and followed, I-"

A nearby officer stopped him short, "Sir, sir- it seems there was some sort of earthquake on the property. We are trying to evacuate the area as soon as possible."

"We're going to take her in, her lung capacity is compromised, and we won't know how bad some of these cuts are until we get her cleaned up," Declared one of the EMTs, "hop in if you want to ride with us."

Dad immediately jumped into the back, the doors shut, and the sirens signaled we were leaving. As we descended the drive, I watched Grayson Estate fade from view.

A few weeks later, we received a thick envelope from the lawyers. The packet informed us that, as a result of the events that unfolded, I was the sole proprietor of the Grayson Estate, and if I would be so kindly as to set up a meeting with them at my earliest convenience to discuss my inheritance. I called them that afternoon.

"Would you be willing to come to the estate to discuss this further next Tuesday? We have had top geologists clear the land, so there is no worry about another disaster." the lawyer said with a hearty chuckle.

"Honestly, I'd prefer to never see that place again. Can you get rid of it?" I inquired.

"Bu-But it has been in your family for generations!" he sputtered, "and in light of recent events, it might be difficult to get on the market. We would- *you* would suffer a huge loss if you sold now." He was clearly getting out of breath.

"I don't care if you have to give it away." I answered coldly.

"Young lady, I don't think you appreciate the heritage, the

tradition-" at this, I cut him off.

"You're right, I don't appreciate any of that. I guess I'm just cut from a different cloth, and *I think* that's a good thing

BAKU

Peggy Christie is an author of horror and dark fiction. Her work has appeared in dozens of websites, magazines, and anthologies, including *13 Little Hells*, *Necrotic Tissue*, and *Fearotica: An Anthology of Erotic Horror*. You can find her short story collections, *Dark Doorways* and *Hell Hath No Fury*, from Dragons Roost Press, and her vampire novel, *The Vessel*, from Source Point Press. Peggy is an officer, and one of the founding members, of the Great Lakes Association of Horror Writers, as well as a contributing writer for the websites of Cinema Head Cheese and Slack Jaw Punks. Check out her webpage at themonkeyisin.com for more information on her other publications, and appearances. Peggy loves Korean dramas, survival horror video games, and chocolate (not necessarily in that order) and lives in Michigan with her husband and their dog, Dozer

R D Doan enjoys writing works of dark fiction and horror but has written various academic articles as a Physician Assistant for his "day job" as well. He is an avid reader of nearly all genres but just can't seem to get away from the dark corners of the horror world. He lives in West Michigan with his wife, two sons and dogs; and when you can't find him working or in a book, he's probably out enjoying nature by resting in a hammock or exploring the trails

Max Carrey currently lives in sunny California, but will be moving to a gloomier location much like the settings in her stories (hopefully without the tragedy and mayhem involved). She's had stories appear in Zimbell House's *The Dead Game* and *Spirit Walker*. Chipper Press' *The Princess*. As well as upcoming releases with: PCC

Inscape Magazine and Impulsive Walrus. To stay up to date follow her at: instagram.com/maxcarrey/

Clark Roberts writes horror. His collection *Led by Beasts* has been compared to the earliest works of Stephen King; Roberts is very proud of that comparison. He also has a YA novella titled, *Halloween Night on Monster Island*. Besides reading and writing, Mr. Roberts enjoys the outdoors. He particularly enjoys fishing Michigan trout streams at dusk, when the waters whisper and eyes pop open in the surrounding forests.

Radar DeBoard is a horror movie and novel enthusiast who resides in Wichita, Kansas. He occasionally dabbles in writing and enjoys to make dark and exciting tales for people to enjoy. He has had drabbles and short stories published in various electronic magazines and anthologies.

Aaron Grierson is a commercial support officer at a Canadian bank by day, and a writer at night. He is a contributing editor for *The Missing Slate* magazine, where his essays typically examine the intersection of technologies and their effect on culture. An enthusiastic student of life, he enjoys researching trivia as much as he does for essays or fictional projects. A sense of existential dread drives his search for meaning in an ever-changing landscape of thoughts, memes, politics and fiction. An avid love for reading and gaming helped foster a deep sense of wonder for the speculative - past, present and futures. His fiction and poetry spans history, science fiction, fantasy, horror and the comic.

Some of the tales in **David Allen Voyles'** collections of original horror stories, *The Thirteenth Day of Christmas* and *Tales from the Hearse* were those he told while conducting tours for his ghost tour company, *Dark Ride Tours* in Asheville, NC. Playing the role of gravedigger/storyteller Virgil Nightshade, Voyles entertained guests as they were transported to various spooky sites in a 1972 Cadillac hearse converted for that purpose. Having taught literature for thirty years, Voyles is no stranger to weird tales and horror fiction in general. His love for authors such as Ray Bradbury, Stephen King, Anne Rice, Shirley Jackson, and Neil Gaiman as well as a lifelong obsession with Halloween ensured that it was just a matter of time before he published his own tales of terror. In addition to publishing his stories in print, he is also the creator of the horror podcast, *Dark Corners*, a bi-weekly program of original horror stories which can be found on your favorite podcast app

On just about every rainy evening, you can find **Elias Baum** scribbling away at his writing desk, basking in the atmosphere, listening to the wind, and relishing every dark twist he can work into his tales. When he's not writing, he's busy venturing into the veiled land of dreams, unlocking its mysteries, searching for the silver key. If you've found any clues as to its whereabouts, leave a note for him by the bleeding willow tree. You know the one. Several writers he takes inspiration from, and stores in glass bottles on wooden and dusty shelves, are Soren Narnia, Jorge Luis Borges, Yann Martel, and Oscar Wilde.

Zachary Finn: My short fiction has been published in the anthology, *Hidden Menagerie*, by Dragon Roost Press and in the anthology, *The Monsters We Forgot*, by Soteira press. I also have a short story scheduled to appear in the upcoming anthology, *Hollow 5*, by Breaking Rules Publishing, and I've been featured on horrortree.com in their weekly "drabble" fiction. In addition to my fiction writing, I have a co-authored nonfiction article published on 11/20 for the American Alliance of Museums website and a recent original historical piece published by the New York History Review.

Jen Sexton-Riley is a speculative fiction writer. Born in rural New York, she found inspiration in a five-century-old sea goddess temple on the South China Sea and in the shadows of the world's southernmost subpolar forest. A Clarion West 2018 graduate, she proofreads an indie newspaper and lives by the sea with her partner and daughter. Her work has appeared in *Daily Science Fiction, The Colored Lens, Bewildering Stories,* and *Obscura: An Urban Fantasy Anthology*. Her work will appear in 2020 in *Ghostlight: The Magazine of Terror, Illumen, The Weird and Whatnot,* and elsewhere.

Neil Willoughby is a writer and award-winning filmmaker from St. Clair Shores, MI.

J.M. Van Horn thwarts criminals during the day and writes a blend of horror and urban fantasy at night. His incredible wife and amazing son are his driving force and his absolutely absurd dreams and/or nightmares help fuel him. There are endless levels of horror and you should take time to explore them.

His published works can be found in places like *Sirens Call, Erie Tales,* and *Ghostlight, the Magazine of Terror*.

ABOUT GLAHW

Great Lakes Association of Horror Writers (GLAHW) is a collective and compendium of writers, fans, and misshapen children all huddled together to share their love of Horror, Dark Fantasy, Sci-fi, True Crime, and the occasional Horrotica. We love words to death.

Recurring Nightmares is an annual publication dedicated to making the name of one lucky raffle winner absolutely miserable.

The Raffle is held at the Annual Monster Mash for Literacy Bash, and the proceeds from it and the party are generously donated to the Dominican Literacy Organization of Detroit.

For more information on our group, activities and where to donate bail money, please visit us:

Facebook: https://www.facebook.com/GLAHW
Instagram: https://www.instagram.com/glahw666/
Twitter: https://twitter.com/GLAHW
Website: http://www.glahw.com

Made in the USA
Monee, IL
18 January 2021